Barrie Skelcher is a life-long sailor and sail-racing enthusiast who has, together with the professionals, designed and built sailing and motor cruisers in his spare time. His career in the power generation industry took him from Dounreay, where he researched radiation-induced chemical reactions, to the CEGB and Sizewell A nuclear power station in Suffolk, where he was responsible for safety procedures and later managed information centres for the public and the media in relation to the Sizewell B project. His interest in how uranium is used in the manufacture of coloured glass has led to the publication of two books on the subject. He lives in Suffolk and divides his time between sailing and writing.

By the same author

By a Slender Thread (Navigator Books, 1995)

THE DAY ENGLAND DIED

Barrie Skelcher

Book Guild Publishing
Sussex, England

First published in Great Britain in 2014 by
The Book Guild Ltd
The Werks
45 Church Road
Hove, BN3 2BE

Typesetting in Sabon by
Nat-Type, Cheshire

Printed and bound in Great Britain by
4edge Ltd, Hockley, Essex

A catalogue record for this book is available from
The British Library.

ISBN 978 1 909716 13 1

To all my colleagues who were employed by the Central Electricity Generating Board and who contributed to it being a world leader in the generation and transmission of electricity – before it was broken up by privatisation.

Thank you to my wife, Shirley, and my daughter, Angela, for their suggestions and work in proof reading and checking my spelling and grammar. Without their efforts this book would have been a shambles.

Barrie Skelcher

Author's Note

The population of the world is expanding so quickly that it is outstripping the resources necessary to sustain it. The result is growing tension between different countries and cultures. Conflict, in one form or another, is multiplying as disputes over territories, religions and diminishing essential minerals come to the fore. The presence of nuclear weapons may well deter the outbreak of war on the scale of WWII, but local skirmishes and revolutions will continue to be the order of the day.

The situation will be complemented by terrorist action, as highly motivated individuals and gangs take undercover action at a local level. There have already been many examples across the world and in particular in the most developed countries. Britain comes into this category.

This story is entirely a work of fiction and the names used, whether they be for persons or many of the places, are purely imaginary. They should not be construed as making implications against any real person, organisation or industry. The nationality and ethnicity assigned to the terrorist characters are not significant and should not be construed as such. It is a fact that throughout the world some people, for various reasons, have come to hate Britain. The characters I have used do not necessarily represent the populations of the countries to which I have assigned them. However the story is feasible and for that reason, in some instances, real and realistic locations have been included in the story.

The purpose of this yarn is to illustrate how terrorist gangs could form and operate, and how easy it is to be fooled by their circumstance. Also, how the ordinary citizen can help to thwart impending terrorist activity by cooperating closely with the security authorities and reporting things that don't seem quite right. It also illustrates how such efforts can be frustrated by modern communications and difficulty in making urgent contact with the right person.

Although the story is fiction, the technology is not. Events like this could happen, and might well happen if the policy of concentrating electricity generation in just a few places, instead of making it more general throughout the country as it used to be, is continued.

The photographs are included to give the reader, who might not be familiar with the type of boats and locations relevant to this story, a realistic impression of the settings for the action.

Richard Harry England's boat *Rose of England*

What is an RIB?

For those not familiar with boating terms an RIB is a Rigid Inflatable Boat.

Below is a picture of a typical RIB although it is *not* the one referred to in this story. This boat would have been larger and would have had two engines. The sponson is the inflatable tube that is attached to the rigid hull and keeps the boat afloat. The hull may be made from aluminium, fibreglass, or wood. The sponson is usually made from a polyester coated fabric and is strong but pliable and can be pressurised to form a rigid tube around the hull.

1

15 June 202X
Hitching a Lift

It was late afternoon on a day in mid June. Richard Harry England – known as Dick or 'Blighty' to his friends – sat at the helm of his forty-foot motor cruiser *Rose of England* as it ambled down the Canal de Calais. On either side the canal was lined by trees, behind which lay open country.

For more than sixty years, Richard had been drawn to the waters and boating. In his youth he had been a successful dinghy helm and then in his mid forties he turned to cruising, first under sail but now under power. Although living near Woodbridge in Suffolk, his favourite cruising area was the Near Continent. Over the years he had visited the Baltic but his favourite waters were in Holland, Belgium and France.

Now in his mid eighties, though, he was mulling over the thought that his boating days were drawing to a close. This would probably be his last cruise on the Continental inland waterways and once back in England he would have to contemplate selling his beloved *Rosie*, as he called his boat. It was unusual in design. He had thought up the idea and had the boat built to suit his purpose. *Rose of England* was designed for both sea going and pottering on canals and rivers. The boat had three engines: two small 40 horsepower wing engines which gave the boat superb manoeuvrability at low speeds, and a hefty 400 horse-power main engine for use in open waters.

As he and his crewman Rodney motored slowly along the canal, Dick's thoughts drifted back to events of thirty-five years before. Dick had retired from the nuclear power industry then, but later became involved again when one of the employees at a special establishment set up to store plutonium became suspicious that some of the plutonium was being stolen. When her concerns were rejected by her employees, she recruited Dick and his daughter Sally to help. The climax came when the terrorists obtained a nuclear weapon. In a desperate attempt to stop them exploding it in Den Helder, Dick had rammed another yacht which was carrying the weapon. In the chaos the terrorists managed to fire just one shot. The bullet had ricocheted off the mast and struck Sally in the chest. She had died in his arms. Now he wished that she could have been with them enjoying this final trip.

At the end of the previous season, which Dick had spent cruising in Holland, he had intended to bring *Rosie* back from the Continent but the weather had intervened. Autumn gale after gale had kept *Rosie* bottled up in a Dunkirk marina. Finally he had given up and *Rosie* had wintered out ashore. In the spring, which was blessed with better weather, rather than bring his boat straight back to the Suffolk river where her mooring lay he had indulged in yet another short cruise through the Belgian and French canals. Rodney, who had been Sally's fiancé and was with them on that fateful trip, was now crewing *Rosie*. He had served in the SAS and then had set up as a private investigator. Now in his sixties and retired, he was enjoying spending a few weeks with the chap who might once have been his father-in-law.

From Dunkirk they had travelled along the Canal de

Furnes and on to Nieuwpoort where they refuelled. The weather was set fair and Dick had mulled over the possibility of making a crossing back to England. After discussing it with Rodney he had decided to continue and enjoy the peaceful canal country which is so different from the rough and tumble of a sea passage.

They had made their way along the IJzer to Diksmuide and spent a couple of days moored to the town's quay. On the opposite side of the canal was the towering war memorial which they explored. After climbing to the top they had a magnificent view of the surrounding country which was flat and crossed with waterways. A montage of pictures showed what the area would have been like when, for defensive reasons, it had been flooded. This and the other displays brought back Dick's childhood memories of the Second World War, provoking thoughts of why human beings had to indulge in the process of killing each other.

Leaving Diksmuide, *Rosie* had motored down the

Kanaal Ieper-IJzer to the historic town of Ieper which the British call Ypres. At the end of the Ieper Canal they had tied up in the old town's harbour which in past years would have been serving the canal barges but was now devoted to pleasure craft. A ten-minute walk away was the town itself with a large museum devoted to past wars, and many shops selling war memorabilia. Ieper had held out as a salient into the German lines during WWI and was completely devastated. Churchill had suggested it be kept in its state of ruin as a memorial, but the local people had different ideas and had rebuilt their town. In the evening, Dick and Rodney witnessed the ceremony of the sounding of the 'Last Post' at the Menin Gate. This had been rebuilt as a British War Memorial in the 1920s on the site of the former city gate. On its wall were inscribed the names of fifty thousand British and Commonwealth soldiers who were reported missing in the Great War.

With time ebbing away they returned to Dunkirk via the Lokanaal and Canal de Furnes. Dick's nostalgia meant he wanted to see Calais again, so instead of locking out to the harbour marina they remained in the canal. The next two days were spent ambling along the waterways, the last of which was the Canal de Calais. Little did they know that this apparent small change of plan was to have far-reaching consequences.

They were heading for home, intending to spend the rest of the summer in British waters. It would probably have made for a better crossing to have set out from Dunkirk, but Dick's fond memories of this famous old French port had prevailed. So here they were, motoring slowly down the Canal de Calais only a few kilometres from the Carnot Lock which would let them out to sea. They would spend the night in the canal then next morning slip into the harbour and, weather permitting, make their passage back to the east coast of England.

'I think we'll lie over there,' Dick called out to Rodney, who was already busy in the bow preparing the fenders and lines. Rodney looked back and gave Dick a thumbs-up. Dick nudged *Rosie* over to the port side canal bank which had a concrete frontage and a few bollards. As was not uncommon on the French canals, it was free parking and there was even a tap for fresh water and a point for electricity. As *Rosie*'s bow came within inches of the bank Rodney stepped ashore with bow line in hand and made it fast. Dick put the helm hard over to starboard, pushed the port throttle ahead and the starboard one astern. *Rosie* swung her stern into the side and Dick flicked the stern line to Rodney who made it fast. They were settled in for the night.

'Oh shit,' Dick exclaimed as he glanced over to the other side of the water.

'What's the problem?' Rodney first looked at Dick then followed his line of sight. About a hundred yards from the canal bank there was an area of trees and shrubs; dotted among these were a tatty assortment of small tents and makeshift shelters.

'Now I know why there are no other boats lying here. That must be one of the hideaways for the asylum seekers.' For a moment Rodney looked puzzled. 'They're just waiting to jump a lorry or even a boat to smuggle themselves into the UK.'

'Aw, don't worry Dick, they ain't going to jump this ship. If they try they'll find out I haven't forgotten my SAS training. They'll exit a damned site faster than they got on board,' Rodney responded with a smile. 'We don't need to leave old *Rosie*, we can eat on board then kip down having locked the hatches,' he added.

The pair went down below and rustled up a meal of bacon, fried eggs, and mashed potato. They went up on deck to enjoy a glass of French plonk. Dusk was replacing the setting sun. Their idle minds were interrupted by a voice from ashore.

'You come from England?' a chap was asking. He was of medium height and slim build. The colour of his skin indicated he was probably from the East.

'Yes,' Rodney responded ahead of Dick. 'What's that to you?'

'Ho, I am English, well British. It is nice to meet my fellow countrymen.'

Rodney and Dick glanced at each other, then Dick asked, 'What part of the UK do you come from?'

'I don't know yet, but I have a friend living in the London area who is waiting for me.'

Dick and Rodney mused over this ridiculous reply – they were not going to be party to helping an illegal immigrant beat the UK Frontier Control, but the stranger continued, 'I originally come from Afghanistan.' He had a good command of English, but his accent clearly indicated he was a stranger to the language. 'I worked for the British forces by penetrating the Taliban and was able to report on a couple of ambushes they planned for the Brits. When the Taliban found out it was me who betrayed them I was lucky to escape. The British were very good to me and the Embassy arranged for me to have political asylum. They gave me a new identity and a British passport.' He paused for a few moments to let his words strike home then took a passport from his pocket and waved it at the two British sailors. 'I had to choose a new name so I am now George Monarch. I chose the name after your last king.'

'Ah well, have a nice day,' Dick responded with a note of sarcasm in his voice.

'Are you going to England tomorrow?'

'Yes, what's that to do with you?' Rodney interjected

'I was hoping you would be able to help me,' the fellow continued. 'I want to get to England to my friend. I have no money for the ferry. The British give me money when they give me the passport but I was robbed, now I have no money. Could I work my passage on your boat?'

Dick's first reaction was to reject the request out of hand, but the fellow had a note of sincerity in his voice and his story seemed so improbable that it could be true. For a few moments he mulled over the request, then shot a glance at Rodney.

'You're the skipper,' Rodney said with a wry smile.

Dick tugged at the lobe of his ear while he thought, then looking the stranger straight in the eye demanded, 'Give me your passport. If it's in order I'll have a think. But if I did give you a passage I would have to declare your presence to the frontier control when we arrive in the UK. This is because you did not start the cruise with us.' Dick wasn't sure of the procedure but he reckoned that if the fellow was not genuine the thought of being handed over to the British authorities when they arrived would cause him to back down.

'That is no problem. The Embassy told me when I left that my passport would be accepted without question, but if it was not I was given a secret code word to use that will prove I am genuine.'

'What's the magic word?' Rodney demanded.

'I must not say,' the fellow persisted. 'It is not that I do not trust you, your boat flies an English flag, but I must not use this word except to an area commander.'

For a couple of minutes Dick mulled over the situation. If the chap had worked for the British, risking his life in the process, then he could hardly deny him this request. Was he genuine? Dick had no way of being sure but if the chap was handed over to the authorities when they landed then what harm could there be? At the very worst Dick might have to take the fellow back to Calais but that would be a good excuse for another trip.

'OK George,' he said. 'We sail at seven thirty prompt in the morning for the east coast. I will probably have to take you into Harwich to clear immigration. If you want to come with us you must be here at seven o'clock and you must give me your passport. I presume you have some-where to sleep tonight because you cannot sleep on board this boat.' He was making things a little hard for the fellow and taking no chances. There was no way he would allow a stranger on board while they were asleep.

'Oh, thank you sir,' the fellow replied. 'I will be here as you say. I will have a little luggage with me, just my ruck-sack with my spare clothes and a few memories of Afghanistan.'

Dick nodded, and the stranger turned, waved, and walked away. Dick watched him make his way along the canal bank to the footbridge then cross over and disappear in the wooded area on the other side.

*　　*　　*

Dick did not see the fellow crawl into a small tent, reach into his rucksack and take out a mobile phone. He punched in a number then spoke. 'I have fixed it, should be coming on a motor boat called *Rose of England*. They will want to take me into Harwich to Immigration. Make sure that you are playing the FC game. I will let you know our progress, so make sure you are ready for me.'

It was 07.25 hours the next morning and *Rose of England* was all set to go. The weather forecast for Dover and Thames had predicted a gentle force 2 westerly which would give them a smooth passage. The engines were ticking over and Dick was at the helm on the afterdeck when the stranger arrived.

'May I come on board now?' he asked.

'Once you have handed me your passport,' Dick responded.

George Monarch handed over the document as he stepped aboard. 'Do we leave now?' he asked.

Dick ignored the question. 'Get your gear stowed below, in the fo'c'sle – that's the sharp end of the boat,' he added with a note of sarcasm.

'I know,' George responded. 'I am used to boats.'

Dick gave Rodney a nod and he slipped the bow line as Dick let go aft. *Rosie*, under her wing engines, slipped slowly through the water heading for the lock. The gates were open, so they entered and hooked their fore and aft lines over the bollards. Dick went ashore with ship's papers so that the keeper could log them out. When he was back on board the sluices opened and *Rosie* dropped a metre or so as Rodney and Dick eased the lines. The front gates opened and *Rosie* slid out into the salt water of the inner harbour. Dick fired up the main engine and held *Rosie* on station until the harbour entrance light gave them permission to leave. As they cleared the breakwater,

Rodney took the helm and turned *Rosie* to port, taking her along the approach channel, following the course displayed on the satnav screen.

'Which way do we go?' George asked.

'Go and see Dick, he's in the saloon, he'll show you on the chart.'

The passenger did as he was advised and Dick laid out the old Imray C30 chart he was still using.

'When we get to the end of this approach channel we will set a north east course to cross the shipping channels at right angles. However the tide will carry us north towards the South Goodwin, then we keep clear of the Goodwins,' Dick explained, running his finger along the route. 'We then head up towards the Kentish Knock, probably leave it to port and onto the Long Sand Head North Cardinal mark. After that we bear away to the north east heading towards Roughs Towers. As I have you on board we'll pick up the Cork Sand Beacon and follow the channel into Harwich where you can get clearance to land.'

'How long will it take?'

'I don't intend to burn a lot of fuel so we will toddle along at about nine knots, probably be off the Roughs in about nine or ten hours' time.'

'Thank you very much. It is most kind of you to go out of your way for me,' George responded. 'I would like to thank you sometime. Do you have a phone number or an email address so I can contact you when I have settled down?'

Dick thought for a moment then handed the fellow his card with the details. 'Here,' was all he said, as he turned to go up on deck to join Rodney at the helm. He did not notice George go into the fore cabin, reach into his rucksack and take out his mobile phone. He needed to make the call before they got out of phone range. He punched in the same numbers as he had on the previous evening and when he got a reply simply said, 'We will be off Roughs in about nine hours' time, then we must play the FC game. Good, see you then.'

It was a smooth crossing with a light south-westerly breeze flowing with the tide. Dick and Rodney took it in turns to helm and to plot their course. Dick was one of the old-fashioned skippers – although he would rely on the satnav to show their course and position, he marked off each way point on the chart just in case the electronics failed. They saw a line of broken water as they passed the Kentish Knock then picked out the Long Sand Head North Cardinal and headed towards the Sunk and South Shipwash. The Rough's platforms came into sight.

Much to Dick's surprise he saw a black RIB speeding towards them. Through the glasses he discerned that two chaps in black suits were aboard. On the side of the sponson were the letters UK FC. He throttled back as the RIB made to come alongside.

'Stop your engine,' one of the fellows hailed. 'We are Frontier Control, where are you from?'

'Calais,' Dick replied.

'We will come aboard and check your papers.'

'Be my guest.'

Rodney, who had now joined Dick, took the bowline from the RIB and put a turn round the forward cleat. By now Dick could see the chaps were wearing dry suits and auto-inflatable life jackets, which explained why he could not see their uniforms. One of them stepped up the boarding ladder that Rodney had lowered.

'May I see the ship's papers?' the Frontier Control fellow asked.

'Here,' said Dick as he handed over the certificate of registry, the certificate for insurance, and a receipt for the last fuel he had taken on board at Nieuwpoort. Then he added, 'Glad to meet you chaps. I've got a passenger on board. Picked him up in Calais after he told me a sob story about being stranded without any money for the ferry. He has a valid British passport but I thought you guys ought to check him out so I was going to bring him into Harwich.'

'Can I see him? I must also examine his passport,' the Frontier Control man responded just as George happened to come up on deck.

'I am here. I think you want to see this,' he said as he handed over his passport.

The Frontier Control man examined it, pulled a bit of a face then said, 'Well it looks in order but I am not convinced.' He looked George straight in the face. 'How can you prove this is not a forgery?' he asked.

'I have a special password but I am only able to give it to the head man. It is top secret for special refugees like myself.'

'Well that's a new one on me. I think I will have to arrest this ship.'

Dick winced and was about to make some protest when Rodney intervened. 'Look here, everything's in order. You can search the ship if you wish. The only thing that might be a bit irregular is the passenger, so why don't you take him and let us get on with our journey? We're based on the Deben so if there is any comeback you can easily catch up with us.'

The official paused for a moment as if he was thinking out the situation then responded, 'OK, fair enough.' Turning to George he said, 'Get your gear and make sure you wear the spare lifejacket we have in the RIB.'

George readily agreed, thanked Dick and Rodney then stepped aboard the Frontier Control boat and waved *Rosie* farewell.

The RIB sped back towards Harwich. *English Rose* continued on a north-westerly course for four miles and made up to the red and white buoy marking the entrance to the river Deben. They followed the marks into the river and motored past Felixstowe heading up river past Waldringfield and Methersgate until they picked up their mooring off Kyson Point.

Rodney lowered the inflatable dinghy in its davits while Dick did the usual rounds of closing sea cocks, turning off the electrics and setting the intruder alarm. When all the routines were completed the two climbed down into the dinghy and sculled themselves ashore. Rodney's car was still where he had left it weeks ago in anticipation of their return.

'Well let's hope she starts,' he muttered as he turned the ignition key. The engine fired up and they were on their way to Dick's bungalow just a few miles away. It was a 'between the wars' property in half an acre of land. Dick had extended it when his wife was alive and Sally was a young lass. He also had a large shed which served as a workshop for boat maintenance purposes.

'Going to stay the night?' Dick asked

'Yes, if you'll put up with me,' Rodney responded.

'In that case stop at the chippie in the village and we'll get our supper. I'm too tired to start rustling up our own tucker.'

'Sounds a good idea,' Rodney agreed.

Soon they were at the bungalow, had enjoyed their cod and chips and were having a night cap before turning in.

'That fellow George was a bit odd,' Dick remarked. 'Still the Customs guys took him away, so if it wasn't OK I guess I'll be hearing from them in the near future. Strange though, when I handed the FC guy the ship's papers he didn't seem very interested. He never asked for our address, so even if that fellow George was an illegal immigrant I doubt if we will hear any more.'

13

2

16 June 202X
Meeting at the Chapel

As the RIB pulled away from *Rose of England* George muttered to his companions, 'Thanks, seems to have worked well. The UK Frontier guys have got my description. I'm number one on their wanted list, and I'd have had no chance of getting to you the conventional way. The passport is pretty good but would not withstand a full examination. It fooled that stupid England fellow and his mate anyway.'

As the RIB got closer to the shore and *Rosie* faded into the distance, one of the crew reached over the sponson and peeled off the white self-adhesive lettering. Now they were just a local RIB out for a fun trip. They entered Harwich on the south side and made their way up the Stour to Wrabness. The RIB was run up onto the beach, loaded onto a trailer and attached to the waiting car. With no one else about they were clear away unseen.

Twenty minutes later they reached their destination, a lonely disused chapel in the Suffolk countryside. The trio entered the building through the traditional porch. It still had the layout of a chapel but the pews on the left had been heaped to one side to make room for five camp beds. On the right-hand side there was an assortment of chairs, an old wooden table and a small camping gas stove. The original water supply was simply a cold tap over an old enamelled sink. The RIB crew stripped off their dry suits as they entered. George Monarch followed and all three joined the other two seated round the table. Monarch opened the discussion.

'I will introduce myself. I have been sent by the Leader to take charge of this operation. It will be dangerous but not suicidal. We are here to wreak revenge upon the British nation and, if the opportunity arises, destroy England. Or we will just settle for London. In a way I feel a little sorry for the English as they are dominated by London and ruled by London as if they were Victorian servants. They have done massive harm to our countries, now they must be punished. I know we all have different backgrounds but we can still work together. We will start by introducing ourselves.' He looked round at the others as they nodded in agreement.

'I am from Afghanistan and fighting for the Taliban who one day will regain control of their country now that the British and Americans have gone. I have a passport in the name of George Monarch, which is the name that will be used all the time I am here. For security reasons we will not reveal our real names, not even to each other. I have considerable experience of setting up revenge operations. Unfortunately I am known to the British anti-terrorist police as I spied on the British by working for them in Afghanistan.' He paused for a moment and turned to the man next to him who had been the skipper of the RIB. 'Your turn.'

'I am from Iraq. I was involved with the chemical warfare group. I hate the British for what they did. My country is now in ruins and all we held sacred has been destroyed. I have a forged British passport and go under the name of Alan Everyman. I am very good with explosives and chemistry.' He paused and his companion from the RIB spoke.

'I come from the Emerald Isle and will do whatever is needed to get rid of the British and their Protestant ideas. They are poison in our land. I can also handle explosives and use an assault rifle as the English already know to their cost. My name over here is Charles French.' He nodded to the chap next to him, 'Your turn.'

'I am from Libya, I want revenge for what the Americans and the British did to our beloved leader Colonel Gaddafi. I was a major in his army. My name here is Stephen Ridup. You next.'

The last of the quintet had his say. 'I am from west *Deutschland*, I believe you call it Germany now. My grandfather was commandant of one of the prisons where the traitors of the Third Reich were held. When the British came they threw him to the inmates who tore him to pieces. I know that to be true because my father told me. Hitler knew what the world needed; it was the new order of National Socialism. That is what we need now and the first step must be to destroy the selfish capitalist system of which Britain is the heart. My name here is James Unnot.'

'Right, now we know each other.' George Monarch resumed and took charge of the meeting. 'I will review the situation. This property has been bought in the name of Charles French. It was thought someone with a genuine Irish accent would attract least attention. It was chosen as it is in a remote area and has planning permission to be converted to a dwelling.

'Our comings and goings will be accepted by any locals who notice us. They will think we are working on the conversion. However we must observe the tightest security. My leader thinks the British authorities are worrying that another terrorist attack is on its way. He has warned me that the security forces will be monitoring mobile phone calls and emails, intercepting written mail and have their informers just about everywhere. We will need to contact each other and send messages so we must disguise them. We will call our base, this place here, "Desert Island". Collectively we will be the "Musketeers", so if we arrange a meeting like this you would get a message something like "the musketeers are meeting for a session of desert island discs". Anyone eavesdropping would think it was some little known pop group having a music session. Get the idea?'

The others nodded, and their leader continued, 'We will not use the names we have now adopted but disguise them by referring to some film or television character. Commit the following to memory, do not write anything down.' He gave a quick smile and continued. 'I am George Formby, who was a popular singer and comedian during and after World War Two. Alan Everyman, you are Alan Banks from the TV detective series *DCI Banks*. Charles French you are Charlie Chaplin, a popular film star comedian during and after World War Two. Stephen Ridup, you are The Saint, Simon Templar, a do-gooder who could outwit or out-fight any baddie he came across. It was a popular TV series about fifty years ago. James Unnot, you are John Steed from *The Avengers*, an old TV series; if you want to know more use Google.'

He waited until the others all nodded. 'Don't use the names directly: don't say "I have arranged to meet George Formby tonight". Use a bit of finesse such as "I have arranged for a session of George Formby songs tonight". Got the idea?' They each nodded in turn. Their leader paused to allow them to digest what had been said, then continued, 'We still have to devise our plan. We must launch an attack that will put 9/11 in the shade. We want to paralyse the whole of Britain in one swoop and to make our getaway unscathed. What are your ideas?'

The short silence that followed was broken by the Libyan Stephen Ridup.

'I understand that the British have to import their gas and do so in large tankers coming into port in South Wales. If we were to put a missile into one of those ships there would be a massive explosion that would close the port and leave the country short of gas.'

Allan Everyman cleared his throat. 'I don't think it would be that easy. Yes you would sink the ship, probably set it on fire, but a gas cloud explosion would first require a lot of the gas to escape before it ignited. Perhaps,' he paused for a moment in thought, 'if the missile had a non-explosive warhead so that it just punctured the hull and caused the gas to escape, then after a little time an explosive was fired, a gas cloud explosion would be possible. The timing would be critical.'

George Monarch intervened. 'The idea has possibilities. I agree with Alan there are difficulties but I think it is worth further investigation. Suggest you take James, go over to Wales, talk to the locals, find out all you can about these gas vessels then report back. We may have a problem in getting a suitable missile but we will worry about that nearer the time.'

James now spoke. 'George, I was going to suggest we had a go at the water supplies. Remember the Dam Busters in World War Two and the chaos that their attack caused? I know we don't have aircraft and bouncing bombs but there are possibilities.' He paused, looked round at the others who looked bemused, then continued. 'Some of the big cities get their water supplies from artificial reservoirs in Wales. I know Birmingham and Liverpool do. Instead of a bouncing bomb we could simply lower a bomb down the side of the dam and time it to explode when we have made our getaway. While we are in Wales investigating the gas ships we could also take a look at the dams, I expect there is a lot on the web about them'

'Good idea,' George responded. 'As the old British

radio star Dick Barton used to say, "Time spent on recce is seldom wasted", so go and do a recce.'

'What about the massive oil refinery on Canvey Island?' Alan Everyman suggested. 'One single missile striking in the right place could start a fire that would spread to all the refineries. We could even attack from the water at high tide; it would be a shame not to use the RIB now we have it.'

George nodded. 'Good thinking, Alan, I will come with you.' He paused again. 'Any other ideas?'

Charles French let out a sigh. 'You guys are missing the obvious target. Not a million miles from here is the largest nuclear power station site in Europe. If we blew up their reactors it would be a Fukushima in Suffolk and Essex, and create chaos in East Anglia.'

'How do you propose we do that?' George asked. 'These sites have very tight security. I understand that the operators only have to press a button and the reactor shuts down. Even if you went in shooting they would be able to shut off the reactor, then how would you cause a nuclear release?'

'Dunno, but if we figure it long enough I guess we could work out a way of doing it. Who knows, I might even get a job there. I've heard they take on temporary staff during their overhaul period. I'll suss it all out while you guys are gallivanting. I can operate from here and someone ought to stay and occupy the place. After all I am supposed to be the owner!'

The meeting came to an end and each of the conspirators made their way into a camp bed. The last one to do so turned out the lights.

It was around 7 am when James, the German, was the first to wake. He rolled out of his bed and made for the kettle. Soon the others were up and rustling up their own breakfasts. As they sat round the table George Monarch started to get things moving.

'OK guys, we agreed last night what we were going to do so let's get on.' He turned to James. 'How are you and Stephen going to get to Wales?'

'I'll walk into the village, only take about fifteen minutes. Bloggs and Co, that's the name of the local garage, hire out cars. A week or ten days should be enough. I've got a UK licence, had to take a test a few months ago, so it is quite legitimate if we get stopped. We'll have a spin round Wales as if we are tourists. It is now the time of year people take holidays so we will not arouse suspicions. Holidaymakers are usually curious about the places they visit so there shouldn't be any problems.'

'Sounds good to me, I propose we meet back here no later than 28th June, is that OK?' George asked. He looked round at each in turn and all nodded. 'What about you, Charles?'

'Oh I'll be slinging a few things in the bags and taking the motorbike. I know it has Irish plates but so what? I've got my Irish licence which is legit over here so what the hell?'

'But it will have your real name.'

'Don't matter, I won't be using my real name and I won't be staying anywhere, just out and back each day.'

'OK,' George agreed. 'Alan and myself will take the car. It is registered in Charles's name but insured for Alan so he will have to drive me around. We will give this place Canvey Island a look over, also maybe some other places along the Thames. It would be good if we could attack the Parliament, that would shake the British.'

'You mean do a Guy Fawkes? He was the guy who tried to blow up Parliament years ago.' Charles added.

'Ah yes, that would be a good idea. Could we do it on the anniversary, whenever that is?'

'Well, they say it was 5th November and the English celebrate it by having bonfires and fireworks. Maybe we could make a big bonfire for them,' Charles concluded with a touch of Irish humour.

3

James and Stephen walked down the narrow country lane until they reached the small village garage. The proprietor came out to meet them. 'What can I do for you gentlemen?' he asked.

James, using his German accent, replied, 'We are down here on holiday, staying with my old friend Charles French. He has just bought the old chapel and we are helping him do it up. We thought we would take a week or so off to see something of your country. We have heard a lot about Wales and we'd like to see the valleys. Heard you hire cars, so could we hire one from you?'

'When do you want it? I've only got a Ford with a small engine but it should do you. It's free at the moment.'

'Well we would be happy to start now if we can clear the paperwork.'

'Shouldn't be a problem. Have you got a driving licence?'

'Of course. It is German but under EU rules it should be acceptable here.' James passed over his licence, which was in his true name of Hans Muller. The garage man took it into his office and then returned with a set of forms.

'You must fill these in, including your temporary address. I have made a copy of your licence and under the new rules I have to send the details to the DVLA, but you can take the car now. I will need details of your credit card so I can charge you for the time and distance. These are my rates.' He passed a sheet over.

James glanced at it and simply said, 'OK, let's go.'

They drove back to the old chapel with James getting used to driving on the left side of the road. They picked up their basic kit and an hour later they were on their way to mid Wales. It was a long journey. On the outskirts of Leominster they found a B&B for the night.

The next morning they made a comfortable start, passing through some beautiful country before reaching Rhayader where they had a coffee break in a small café and made some local enquiries about Elan village and the reservoirs that supplied the city of Birmingham with water. A short drive later they stopped for a pie and a pint at Elan, then donned their walking clothes and set out on foot to carry out a surreptitious assessment of the dam. It was not what they had expected. There was no easy access to the vulnerable part and it would be no easy matter to lower a massive bomb over the side. Nevertheless they enjoyed the walk. As afternoon gave way to evening they returned to the village to find another B&B for the night.

Next morning it was again a leisurely start as they headed to Builth Wells then on to Llandovery where they picked up the A40 to Haverfordwest. Stopping just outside the town they played the interested tourist role, visiting pubs and cafes, chatting to the locals and gleaning all they could about Milford Haven, the docks, and the gas terminal. As evening approached, just to allay any suspicions that their enquiries might have aroused, they headed south west towards the coast until they came across a small hotel which had a 'vacancies' sign. They booked in for two nights, explaining that they were on holiday just touring around. Having come from the flat lands of East Anglia they wanted to see the hills and valleys of Wales about which they had heard so much. They also let it be known that they were of the boating fraternity, so were interested in the marinas and harbours around the beautiful Milford Haven. From this they gained a lot of useful background information, including that there was some local concern over the safety of the gas terminal.

Playing the tourist role on the morning of day four, they gave the impression of not being in any hurry to leave. Having picked up some tourist leaflets from the hotel, they drove slowly over to Milford Haven, making notes about the surrounding countryside and suitable places where they could set up base if they were to plan an attack on the terminal. It was a warm sunny day with blue sky and a few white clouds. From the water front, under the pretence of being interested in bird life, they used their binoculars to study as much as they could of the docks.

Their efforts were rewarded as they witnessed one of the large gas tankers making way along the narrow buoyed channel and finally, with the aid of tugs, docking at the terminal. Their minds were full of thoughts of how a hit could best be made. It would be difficult from the shore but from a small motor cruiser it would be easy. The problem then would be how to escape. Perhaps a night assault on a tanker while it was being unloaded was a possibility. Wandering along the promenade enjoying an ice cream, they met up with a chap who had a slight nautical look. He was not in any uniform but was wearing blue trousers and a fisherman's-style smock. They opened a conversation with the line, 'You must be one of the lucky locals living here, what a beautiful country this is!'

The fellow removed his pipe from his mouth and replied in a Welsh accent, 'Yes, it isn't bad, but there are hidden bits we don't like. Those great big tankers out there are a menace; they just can't manoeuvre like the smaller ships. I know, I used to work on them when they were much smaller and not full of this frozen LPG.'

'You mean liquid petroleum gas?'

'Yes'

'Surely the government wouldn't let them come in if they weren't safe?' Stephen replied, then chancing a little indiscretion he added, 'I'm originally from Kuwait. That was a long time ago. I live in England now but I remember the big tankers there and they were always safe.'

'Ah,' the local man replied, 'but that must have been years ago when they carried oil. Now they have this gas, it has to be kept at minus one hundred and sixty degrees to keep it liquid. That isn't easy, just think what would happen if cooling went wrong or the thing had a collision and started to leak. If the gas evaporated it would form a cloud over the town. Well, that is until it exploded like an atom bomb.'

'Do all the local people think like you?' James enquired.

'Not all of them have enough sense. They are more interested in jobs than in safety but one day they will regret it; not in my life time I hope. The Mags did their best to resist the development.' In response to the look of puzzlement on James's face he explained, 'Mags, that stands for the Milford Against Gas campaign. They made strong protests to the government but got nowhere. They pointed out that even if the tankers do have a double hull for safety, an armour-piercing missile from a terrorist would soon make short work of that.'

He paused for breath, then continued, 'Them blasted politicians are only interested in short-term gain. They don't listen to the ordinary folk like us. They just get their ears full from the big boys who want to make a fast buck.' He snorted derisively, then added, 'If these tankers are as safe as they make out, why don't they dock them in London?'

He seemed to pull himself together then, and concluded, 'I shouldn't be talking like this to you tourists. I might frighten you from coming again, and we need the holiday folk to bring a bit of cash into the area. It's the governments, both Welsh and British, that rake in the lolly from this, not us locals, we don't even see the rates they pay. Oh well, enjoy your stay. "Have a nice day" as the Yanks say.'

With that he walked away, leaving the two future terrorists with some serious thinking to do as they made their way back to the hotel.

'Reckon we should book another night at the hotel and spend tomorrow looking for boats and places where they are moored. If we are going to mount an operation from here then we need to take the info back to the Desert Island,' James commented to Stephen, who agreed with a smile.

The next morning they signed out of the hotel and drove to the mouth of the estuary. Starting at St Ann's Head they made their way along, following the shore wherever they could, to Milford Haven then finally crossed the toll bridge to Nayland where they headed back towards England. Around the Haven they had called at numerous boat yards and marinas, and noted a few that might suit their purpose. They had viewed five boats that were for sale at different places. For two they took full details of the boats which would have suited their purpose. As evening closed in they found their night's accommodation just short of Carmarthen.

In the hotel lounge they settled down with a drink to have a chat. James commented to Stephen, 'I think we should report our progress just in case we need to do more before we return'

'Agreed,' Stephen said. 'We've come a long way. We

don't want to have to come back because we've over-looked something.'

James took out his mobile and called George's number. 'Hello,' was all he got by way of response.

'I'm looking for the guy that's leaning on the lamppost at the corner of the street,' James said, trying to put a tone of humour in his voice.

'That's me,' George responded. 'You want to talk about our Desert Island Discs?'

'Yeah, John Steed here, I'm doing the Avengers bit if you remember. Thought I'd let you know that we've been busy rehearsing and have got a good act worked out for the tanker sketch. The blocked-up river sketch we don't think would be appreciated so we've ditched that one.'

'Hi John, good to hear from you. I think one turn will do from your troop. Have you got all the props you need?'

'Well not exactly. One is likely to be a bit pricey – about twenty thousand. I thought we ought to get together and see if we could do it any cheaper or whether we might put on a different show?'

George Monarch caught the gist of the message. They had funds but that would be stretching their resources. They had plenty of time in hand so he replied, 'Yeah, that's pushing the budget. We'll have a show meeting here next week so come over and we'll sort out what we're going to do.'

'OK Mr Formby, keep leaning on that lamppost.' James rang off.

The others had also been busy. George and Alan took themselves off in the car to Canvey Island. They spent the afternoon part driving and part looking around. Much to George's surprise the place was not a huge oil and gas terminal but a rather pleasant holiday town. It was a sunny afternoon and they walked down the High Street and along the Eastern Esplanade passing, and occasionally chatting to, the holidaymakers. They did note that as the tide went out there was a large expanse of dried-out foreshore which would have made an assault from the water difficult other than at high water. As the evening approached they decided to stay the night. A small hotel offering an evening meal and bed and breakfast at a reasonable charge provided their overnight accommodation.

The next morning, although it was not their normal practice, they both chose the full English breakfast option. They were mulling over the previous day's wanderings when the chap who had been serving them appeared to ask if they required more toast. They did not, but George thought it a good opportunity to get some local knowledge. The fellow did not appear to be in a hurry so he commented, 'It's a great place here for a holiday, we've not been before. Heard a lot about it but got the impression that it was all full of oil refineries. You been here long?'

'Yus mate, lived 'ere all me life. I was born just down the road. Not much in the way of well-paid jobs but as you say it's great to be 'ere.'

'Aren't you worried about the danger from all the oil terminals? What if they caught fire or a terrorist blew them up?'

'Nah that ain't a problem. Ain't so many of 'em now as there used to be. Anyhow they're pretty secure and the guys there know 'ow to deal wiv any trouble.' He paused for a moment then added, 'If there was anyfing to be afraid of it's that load darn the river by the Medway.'

'Oh? What's that?' Alan asked.

'Well if yer don't know I ain't gonna tell yer. Anyhow it's all under water. But they say if a terrorist really wanted to cause trouble that would be their target, not 'ere.'

George gave Alan a nudge under the table and chipped

in, 'Well thanks for the warning. We feel quite safe here but we've got to get back to work so we'll have to be leaving soon.'

'Oh, what's yer job then?'

'Us? We're into archaeology up in Scotland. Just having a few days looking around before we make the long drive back; got to go north of Inverness.'

As the man left the table George whispered to Alan, 'Didn't think we should push the matter about that underwater problem after he'd mentioned terrorists. I'll explain later.'

The two got up from the table, paid their bill, collected their belongings and made their way to the car. It was only then that George explained to his co-conspirator.

'The English security services have set up something called "Duckwatch". It's an organisation where local police have made contact with people who use the waterways, live near the coast, or come into contact with tourists and so on. These folk act as eyes and ears for the intelligence services and report anything they think a bit unusual or suspicious to the security services. I didn't think that chap who gave me a lift across the North Sea was one of them – he didn't ask enough questions, was free with information, and was quite happy when I agreed to go through the UK FC. However this guy seemed different – if he didn't have any suspicions why did he not tell us the full story of what's under the water? I'm sure he wanted us to push for more info, which would have confirmed his suspicions, which he would then have reported to Duckwatch. He probably has our car's registration number and that would have led the spooks back to our Suffolk base where it's registered.

'When we get back to base I might give that chap England a call, thank him for his help and if it seems OK arrange to meet him again. I reckon he's done a lot of pottering in these east coast rivers and will probably know what the fellow was referring to.'

That evening, back at their base, George played around on the computer using the search engines to try and find out anything about Richard Harry England and his boat *Rose of England*. There were thousands of entries he had to skip through or search. The search words he keyed in were extremely common but using advanced search facilities he managed to narrow down the results. Eventually he came upon an article England had written for *Motor Boat Britain* magazine, in which he described an east coast cruise from the river Deben up to a marina near London Bridge and back. He also found a report about England's earlier political life, when he had once stood for parliament proclaiming the virtues of democracy and how it hung by a slender thread. There was also a newspaper extract about England being involved in a boating accident in Holland, and how his daughter Sally had been killed.

It was just gone nine thirty the next morning when George dialled the number that Dick England had given him. After only four rings the call was answered.

'Dick England speaking.'

'Ah, Mr England, this is George Monarch. Do you remember, you gave me a lift across the North Sea?'

'Yes, of course I remember. Everything go OK?'

'I would like to thank you for your help, just when I needed it. Everything is OK with me. Those officials who took me ashore were very helpful. They examined my papers and I told their boss my special password. He went away to test it then came back and confirmed my status. They let me use their phone to call my friend who came to fetch me. It all went very well.'

'I'm glad to hear it,' Dick responded in a slightly uninterested voice.

'I will be going to Scotland soon, my friend, and I have a job doing some archaeological digging. It's right up north by Inverness. Before I go I would like to thank you for your help. Could we meet up for lunch tomorrow? My friend has recommended a little pub just outside Woodbridge and I can get there by bus.'

Dick thought for a few moments. He had no commitments so why not take up the offer of a free lunch?

'Yes that would be fine. What's the pub's name and what time?'

'Well the bus gets there at twelve. The pub is the Master and Commander and I am told it has a picture of a ship outside. Will your friend be coming?'

'Yes I know the pub, but Rodney is away at the moment so it will just be me.'

'That is fine Mr England – or may I call you Dick?'

'By all means, George,' Dick responded, placing emphasis on the George. 'See you tomorrow.'

The bus was a few minutes late and Dick was waiting in his car when George Monarch arrived.

'Sorry to keep you waiting,' George apologised.

'Oh that's no problem, let's go inside shall we?'

George went up to the bartender and asked about his reserved table. The chap pointed to one in the corner. George picked up the menu and handed it to Dick. 'What you drinking, and what do you fancy to eat?'

'Oh I'll have a bitter shandy, and ... the pork chops.'

'Good. I will go and order them. I think I will have a fruit juice and fish and chips.' George went over to the bar, placed the order for the food and returned with the drinks. It struck Dick as a bit odd that his host was just having a soft drink in a pub when he was not even driving.

'You have a very nice boat in *Rose of England*, did you build her?'

32

'No,' Dick said, 'but I did design her especially with the three engines. Are you a boating person, you seem quite knowledgeable about them?'

'I know a bit, my father used to work on a little ferry.'

They chatted on for a while, then George steered the conversation the way he wanted. 'You must be very experienced in these local rivers.' Dick nodded and George continued, 'I suppose you know the River Thames very well?'

'I've been down there a few times.'

'It must be a very interesting river with plenty of things to see. Have you been up as far as London Bridge or even the Houses of Parliament?'

'Yes I did go that far once. Parliament actually has water frontage.'

'We could not have that in Afghanistan, it would be too easy for terrorists to attack, but then you don't have that problem in England.'

'Not yet we don't, but come to think of it from that angle Parliament would be a soft target. It is well guarded from the road but I don't know about the water. Never seen any guards there.'

George tried a joke. 'Maybe if your Mr Guy Fawkes had tried from the river he would have succeeded.'

'Maybe,' was all Dick replied.

'It must be a beautiful river, what are your favourite places?'

'Well I like the Sheppey area and the Medway. There are some places of historical interest. You can sail right down to Chatham and see the Historic Dockyard. Then there is the Swale, a tributary off the entrance to the Medway. Often pick up a mooring at Queenborough which is very sheltered. Sheerness stands at the entrance to the Medway and that's an interesting town, although there is an old power station opposite.'

'I suppose you have to know the river very well – there must be a lot of hidden dangers?'

'Not really. The channels are well buoyed to mark the deeper water although boats do sometimes go aground.' Dick paused for a moment then continued, 'There is reputed to be one very nasty hazard near the entrance to the Medway. The Thames Barrier is also something to be alert about just in case they decide to close it.'

'What is the hazard at the Medway?'

'Well, it's supposed to be an old American cargo ship called the *Richard Montgomery*, loaded with explosives, shells and bombs. It ran aground during World War Two and was never salvaged.'

'You mean it is still there?' George asked, trying to conceal his excitement and wondering if this could be the problem that the man at the hotel had mentioned.

'Yes it's still there. There is a difference of opinion amongst the experts as to whether it would be best to try and unload it or just let the explosives settle into the mud. Some argue that a simple accident of a ship running into it could set off a massive explosion but, well, there is an account of a ship that did run into it and nothing happened. Personally I think it's pretty safe as it is, unless some idiot were to drop a depth charge on it but then they would blow themselves to pieces.' Dick paused again, 'Am I boring you?'

'Oh no, please go on. What would happen if it did explode?'

'That's an open question. There have been a few novels written about criminals threatening to blow it up, but no one has tried. Some folk say that the worst time would be at high water as that would send a tidal surge up the Thames and cause massive flooding in London. Might even cause a problem at Canvey Island if there was a tanker in the process of unloading. Other folk fear it blowing up at low water when the blast effect wouldn't be damped down and would be felt in Sheerness, causing a lot of damage. Anyhow, it won't happen. I've cruised there several times and lived to tell the tale.'

At this point the food arrived, and George thought it time to drop the subject in case it aroused suspicions. They enjoyed their food, chatted a little afterwards about the archaeological work in Scotland for which George was destined, then they went their separate ways.

As George sat on the bus taking him back towards the old chapel, he became more and more convinced that the *Richard Montgomery* was what the man at the hotel had had in mind, and that it could make a good target for a terrorist attack. More research on the Internet was required.

Back at the chapel Charles French, the Irish conspirator, set out on his mission. About twenty miles away was a nuclear power station complex, at what used to be the old fishing village of Deephole on the Suffolk coast. He packed some bits and pieces in the panniers of his motorcycle, including books on birds and seashore plants and a pair of binoculars. His plan was to pose as a bird watcher with an interest in plants. It would give him cover while he had a good look at the set-up.

The entrance to the nuclear site was off a road that leads from the nearby town of Munchington to the sandy beach. As he motored past on his way to the beach he noticed the speed bumps on this access road and could just make out a concrete gatehouse. When he reached the beach he parked his bike in the public pay and display car park, picked up his binoculars and started to amble along the beach towards the power station frontage. He noted the double security fence, topped with razor wire. A close examination through the glasses showed detection devices on the wire. Surreptitious access, by cutting the wire or trying to climb over it would be difficult if not impossible.

'Those security people seem to have done a good job,' he muttered to himself. As he lowered his glasses he heard the voice of a stranger who had come up to him unnoticed.

'Hi mate. See anything interesting?' the fellow asked.

For a moment Charles froze, then relaxed a little when he saw the chap had a lady with him and responded, 'Thought I saw an avocet over by that building just behind the wire,' trying to emphasise his Irish accent.

'No way mate. Avocets don't live on concrete – they're waders, root in the mud for their bread and butter.'

Charles tried to recover his composure and smiled at the lady. 'I'm just down here on a holiday break. Not my choice, but I won a prize in a local magazine back in Ireland and it requires me to get as far away from Ireland as I can and list the different birds I see. Must admit I'm a bit of a novice.' He paused for a moment then added, 'What is that place over there? Is it one of those nuclear places that we've banned in Ireland?'

'Yes it is,' replied the lady, 'and we all wish it weren't here.'

Charles raised his eyebrows; this was a situation worth pursuing.

'Oh, and I'm thinkin' that you English folk are all in favour of the nukes. This must be Deephole then, isn't it one of the super-safe latest?'

'That's the crap they'll tell you,' the chap snapped back, 'but we aren't that easily taken in.'

Charles sensed that there could be more to this couple than he first thought, so he probed for more information.

'When you say "we", do you mean just the two of you, or are there others who ...?' He was interrupted by the lady.

'We're on the committee of the local NNN organisation

and we know what we're talking about. The government's so-called experts that make these absurd safety claims are not as independent as they claim. They're paid by the government so they have to say what the government want the public to hear.'

'What is NNN?' Charles enquired.

'Not heard of us?' the lady responded. 'Stands for "No No Nuclear". Want to join us?' She did not wait for an answer but handed Charles a small card with the address of the local NNN branch.

'I suppose you're worried about a terrorist attack setting the place on fire?' Charles asked.

'No, it's not that,' the fellow responded. 'Those guys who operate the place are all keyed up for something like that. They won't openly admit it but the police are all armed. They're not the ordinary coppers but special nuclear police and that's why we think they are armed. There is a double fence and by the time an attacker had cut through the first the security guys would be there shooting. Also even if the terrorists did get in, there is not a lot they could do. The operators would simply shut down the reactors. The reactor building is closed off with special steel doors when the reactor is critical. No, it's not a terrorist attack that worries us.'

'You mean something like Fukushima then?'

'It's simpler than that, tell him Bill,' the lady urged.

'Do you think I should Jane? For all we know he might be a terrorist.' Bill shot a smile at his female companion.

'Oh, don't be bothered about me, I'm no terrorist,' Charles said with a chuckle. 'Must admit some of my fellow countrymen don't like the English but it's only the English in our Emerald Isle that are targeted. But please, don't tell me any more if you're worrying.'

After a nod of approval from the lady Bill resumed. 'No, you don't look like a terrorist to me. Anyhow our worries are common knowledge. It's the Singapore syndrome.'

'What's that?' Charles asked.

'During World War Two the British had a naval base in Singapore. It was very important to them and heavily defended. All their guns were pointing out to sea from where they expected an attack. In the event the Japs took it with ease, capturing thousands of British troops – by attacking from the land. The Brits had concentrated on defending the expected and overlooked alternatives which in the circumstances made them more vulnerable. Well, it's the same with the nuclear power stations; they're heavily defended against a frontal attack but have overlooked their weak point.'

'Which is?'

'See that line of pylons over there?' Bill pointed to a double set of power lines leading from the power station. 'Well if they came down while the stations were on full load it would be a disaster – and they could easily be brought down by an accident with a light aircraft.'

Charles nodded and waited for the chap to continue.

'There is so much power goin' down those lines that the grid wouldn't be able to cope if that amount of electricity was suddenly lost. The system would go unstable and the whole lot could crash, leaving the country without power. It would probably take days to get everything back to normal.'

'Yes, but that would only be a costly inconvenience,' Charles suggested.

'No, it could be much worse than that. When the reactors are shut down in an emergency, which would follow the loss of the transmission lines, they still have to be cooled. They generate a lot of heat from the decaying radioactivity. If they don't get cooled all the water boils away, probably bursting the containment, and the uranium fuel starts to melt releasing a massive amount of deadly radioactivity.'

'Surely the designers must have thought of that?'

'Yes they did, and to cope they installed some standby diesel-powered generators to provide the electricity to work the cooling pumps. See those stacks over there?' He pointed towards the power station. 'They're the exhausts from the diesels. Everything would depend on whether those diesels started as they should. If they didn't it would be Fukushima right here, and at Munchington. Its seven-thousand population and its industrial estates would have to be evacuated pronto. The council wouldn't be able to cope, although they won't admit it, and the locals, poor sods, would be breathing in the contaminated air for hours. With some of the isotopes what goes in doesn't always come out, so for the rest of their shortened lives they would be radioactive. I've no doubt that when some of them started dying of cancer there would be lengthy and costly court battles, like there have been for those chaps who were involved in the weapon tests.'

Bill paused for breath, and Charles probed a little further. 'But surely you are being too pessimistic. Don't they test the diesels?'

'Oh yes, every month. They use quite a lot of diesel because a tanker calls after every test.'

'Well that's OK then, no need to worry. I'll just get on with my bird hunting.'

'It wouldn't be all right though if the diesels got knocked out, perhaps by a terrorist,' Bill responded.

'You seem to know a lot about it, did you work there?'

'No but we get briefed by the NNN.'

'Well, thanks for the info. It has been very interesting talking to you. I'll think on what you've said, especially as there is some talk of using nuclear back home.' With those closing remarks Charles walked away, pretending to be looking for birds until the couple were out of sight.

He walked along the shore, casting glance after glance at the nuclear site. He paused when he came alongside the building with the chimney stacks. It was set back from the fence but appeared to be only lightly clad. Probably a bit too far to lob a hand grenade but a rocket-propelled grenade should have little difficulty in hitting the target. He returned to his motorbike, kick-started the engine and made his way back to the chapel.

By the next morning Charles had had second thoughts and decided to pay another visit to Deephole. As he approached the nearby town of Munchington a brown road sign caught his eye, so he made a detour to the recently built Nuclear Visitors' Centre. It was the size of a large bungalow set at the side of a by-road not far from the site of the nuclear power stations. Inside he signed the visitors' book using a false name and address then wandered round looking at the posters, the models and other display items. It was very comprehensive and covered a wide area of topics ranging from the nature and effects of radiation to a model of the power stations. After browsing for an hour or so, while looking at the power station model he caught the eye of one of the staff and started to ask about some things that a tourist might enquire about. First he asked about the ages of the different stations, who had built them, how many people they employed, etc. He was not interested in the answers but did not want his real objective to become obvious.

'What's that over there?' he asked, pointing to the side of the reactor building model.

'Do you mean that building with the chimney stacks?'

'Yes.'

'That is the diesel generator plant,' the guide responded.

'When the reactor is first shut down it still requires cooling because the isotopes are still decaying and producing heat. The cooling water pumps need electricity which is normally imported via the grid, but if for any reason the grid could not supply, then these diesel generators start up automatically so the site is never without power.'

'Gosh, you guys seem to have thought of everything. Nuclear must be the safest way to generate electricity.' He was leading the guide on and continued, 'Oh but what if the generators don't start, maybe they get a flat battery like a car?'

'It's not like a car; there is a very large bank of batteries with plenty of power to start the generators. In fact they are test run every month and they run for several hours. The electricity they produce gets fed into the grid so it's not wasted.'

'Must use a lot of diesel.'

'Yes quite a lot, that is why the fuel tanks have to be topped up after every test run.'

'My son's in the fuel supply business,' Charles lied. 'What's the lucky company that has the contract? Can any company tender?'

'It's AMMO; they supply many large undertakings in this part of the country. Name stands for Anglia Mega and Minor Oils. Your son's company would be welcome to submit a quote but it's not likely they would better AMMO, they give a very good service. Also as the tanker lorry goes onto site both the company and the tanker driver have to be security cleared'

'That wouldn't be a problem but his company is based in Northern Ireland at the moment. He did say they were looking into starting operations on the mainland so I'll mention it when I next see him. Incidentally where do AMMO operate from, is it Ipswich?'

'No they come from Yarmouth. They are very good,

you can almost set your watch by the time of their arrival. It's all part of the security, first Tuesday at 10 o'clock in the evening. That way they do not get tied up with all the other traffic. They would not be let in if they were not on time, well plus or minus half an hour or so. Also the driver has a unique password which is sent to him before he arrives just in case the IRA try to nobble him,' she replied with a smile, having noted his Irish accent.

'Well I think I must be going now. It has been very interesting and you've convinced me that we should have more nuclear power stations. I will tell my MP when I get back.' With that Charles gave the lady guide a smile and drifted over to the exit. A plan was forming in his mind and now he needed to get back to the chapel. On his way he passed a field across which a line of pylons were marching. He took out his mobile phone and photographed them.

4

30 June 202X
The Plan

The following week the conspirators held their conference in the chapel. They had followed up their research with further background study, often making use of information found on the Internet. Each of the three groups had developed a plan of attack. Their objective now was to decide which of the plans to adopt and how best to put them into action. They each had reservations and it was in their minds that they might have to go back to the metaphorical drawing board.

James and Stephen opened the session with a detailed account of their research and conclusions. James was the spokesperson.

'We had a good look at some of the Welsh dams. We detected a degree of resentment amongst the local population, especially the Welsh nationalists who seem to resent the presence of English second-home owners in the area. If one or more dams could be breached it would have a devastating effect on the local area. Probably cause massive flooding and loss of life, but its impact on the English towns would be uncertain. They all have other sources of water and depending on circumstances might ride out the loss of water without too much upset. However, trying to breach a dam would be a massive project. We would have to construct a bomb of about half a ton or more. I'm not sure just how big it would need to be, would have to do more research and try and get other opinions. We would then have to lower the bomb down the inside of the dam wall so that when it exploded it was at maximum depth where the pressure on the dam is greatest. There was no obvious access place for such an operation although with further research we might find somewhere. We think the practical difficulties of doing this are far too great for our little group. We therefore rule out this option.'

He paused, looked around the others who sat poker faced, then continued. 'We also looked into the possibility of blowing up the water supply pipelines. This we could do at certain points but the authorities would simply close the supply valves. It would be a strong gesture, might even get some local support, but it is not big enough for our present objective. We therefore reject this option.'

He looked round the table and saw others nod in agreement, so undaunted he continued. 'The gas terminal in Milford Haven is a different matter and while there are difficulties we think they could be overcome. We would need a military missile akin to a tank buster, perhaps an old bazooka.'

George interrupted him. 'We don't have one available at the moment but I see no reason why we shouldn't get one, some of our friends backing the expedition should be able to help. Having to get one does slightly increase our risk of discovery but I don't think it should be a holding consideration.'

James accepted the interruption and continued. 'We would also need to acquire a fairly fast motor launch, about thirty feet or so. There are several for sale in the area and money is not a problem to us. The large gas tankers approach the terminal via a four-mile narrow channel. During that approach they are restricted by the depth and cannot easily manoeuvre, so they would be easy to attack from a fast motor vessel. They might also be vulnerable to a shore-launched missile, but it would not be easy to be sure of a clear shot and the range of the missile would need to be greater and more sophisticated. It would complicate the operation. The hulls of these tankers are double skinned, consequently the missile must have considerable penetrating power, hence the need for a bazooka, probably firing a shaped charge.'

He paused again, casting a glance at his Libyan companion who nodded to signify agreement. 'If we had a fast motor cruiser we could zip out as the tanker started its approach, skip round any escort boats pretending to be a curious pleasure craft, then when a hundred yards or so away bring out the bazooka and – bang. We simply turn tail, make for the shore and our escape. We checked some of the boat yards and there are a couple of craft that would suit our requirements up for sale. The one we fancied is an old 1970s Cleopatra with twin out drives. The broker said it will do twenty knots, which would be fine. The boat yard has a pontoon so after the attack we could simply pull onto the pontoon, abandon the boat and make our getaway.'

'Yes but surely you would need to show the boat yard your Boat Master licence before they would let you use their pontoon?' George interjected.

'No they wouldn't. Anyone can drive a boat in the UK, no qualifications required, but we would need to spend some time there with the boat getting used to it before we made the attack.'

'Sounds good,' George interrupted. 'What are the snags?'

'Operationally there aren't any, but the unknown is how devastating the attack would be. The gas is liquid and kept that way at about minus a hundred and sixty degrees, so if the double hull is pierced, liquid gas will squirt out and will have to evaporate before it can explode. From chats with the locals they seem to think the safety services would be able to intervene and prevent a major gas cloud explosion, although we have our doubts. We think a massive fire ball could be created. If so it would certainly make the world's press and increase the clamour for stopping the importing of liquid gas.'

'OK,' said George. 'I'll give our account now, then Charles can tell us what he has uncovered and we will decide which route we want to take. Alan and I went down to Canvey Island, stayed overnight and had a good look round. It was quite disappointing. The locals seemed quite happy and there was not a huge amount of activity around the oil sites. Seems they have reduced since their earlier days. They would not be an easy target and even if we did hit them it would probably not be a great disaster. We don't think this is a worthwhile target.'

He paused and saw a look of disappointment on the faces of the others, cast a glance at Alan who nodded, then continued. 'But in discussion with the waiter at our hotel he referred to a problem on the other side of the river. Wouldn't say what it was other than something by the river Medway which is a tributary lower down the Thames nearer the sea. We thought we might go and have a look round but decided more investigation was required.

'Remember the guy who gave me a lift from Calais? Well I still have his card and as he is obviously a widely experienced local sailor I thought he would know what it was. I took him to lunch as a thank-you for the Channel crossing. He took the bait and we had a chat about the local rivers and the Thames. Seems the Medway has a lot of history with old dockyards and all that, just the sort of thing these Brits go dotty about. He explained that near the entrance to the river Medway a World War Two

46

ammunition ship ran aground and sank. What's more, most of her explosives are still on board. The authorities are too scared to move them as some experts say they will be getting more tender as time goes on.

'There's a lot of speculation about what would happen if the ship blew up. Might send a tidal wave up the Thames and flood London including the Underground. Would probably cause a lot of damage in Sheerness, that's the nearby holiday town. However this chap said it was no great secret; novels have been written about it and, although it is well marked and under surveillance, a ship did run into the sunken wreck but there was no big bang. I got the impression, from the way this chap spoke and what I subsequently read on the Internet, that a small explosive charge would do the trick. Alan reckons he could make something that would do it. The name of the sunken ship is the *Richard Montgomery* so if we go ahead we could call it Operation Alamein.' He paused while the others gave a snigger. 'Right Charles, what have you got for us?'

'Before we go on,' James interrupted, 'I don't like the name Alamein, it's too obvious. How about Clifton James or CJ for short?'

'Where does that come from?' George asked.

'World War Two.' As George looked puzzled, James continued, 'During the preparations for D Day, just to mislead us, the Brits had an actor impersonate General Montgomery and let him be seen well away from the invasion area. It did fool Hitler. If it had not, the result of D Day might have been quite different. The Brits were so cocky about it that they made a film called "I Was Monty's Double" and the role of Monty was played by the actor who did the real impersonation, a chap called Clifton James. Need I say more?'

'No, you need not say another word. We will code name

the operation Clifton James or CJ. Now let's get on.' George responded.

Charles then recounted his investigation on the Suffolk coast, with details of the Deephole nuclear site.

'The nuclear station is pretty secure, it could probably be stormed but not by us few. I think we can rule out an attack on the power stations.' He hesitated as the others pulled faces of disappointment, then with a smirk he carried on. 'We need not attack them – we could wreak havoc without going near them. I met a guy on the beach who was a member of NNN, stands for No No Nuclear, and he explained that the power from the three stations and the North Sea wind generators all goes down one double line of pylons. It is such a large amount of electricity that it could amount to as much as twenty per cent of the total demand for England and Wales. If these transmission lines were suddenly broken then the unexpected loss of power would cause a major problem for the British grid, the system would go unstable and most of England would be blacked out. This would create chaos. It would take several days to get power back again. What is more, this would cause the reactors to have an emergency shutdown and they would then still require cooling. If this was not available, the whole reactor core, you know the uranium, would melt and burn a hole in the pressure vessel. It could even lead to a Fukushima-type accident.'

Alan interrupted him. 'Are you suggesting that all we have to do is to blow up a couple of these pylons? That shouldn't be difficult.'

'Yes. On my way back I took some photos of the pylons. It is not difficult to see that they could be knocked down fairly easily. They are spaced so far apart that there are isolated places where we could get easy access yet bring the wires down on houses or major roads, so adding to the confusion.'

George interrupted him. 'But surely the power stations must be designed to withstand such an accident? It could happen without our help.'

'The chap from the NNN explained this to me. They have standby diesel generators to provide enough power for essential services so that, if they lose the transmission line while they are at full power, these generators provide enough electricity to keep the cooling water pumps going. To create a Fukushima we would have to take out these standby generators without launching any assault on the site. This is how it could be done. The very helpful lady in the nuclear information centre explained that these diesels are run every month and have to have their diesel tanks topped up, always on the first Tuesday in the month at 10 pm. All we would have to do is to contaminate the fuel that is delivered so that when the diesels are fired up they break down. Not quite sure how we do that but there must be a way.'

'Thanks Charles, you seem to have done a good job. Now where do we go from here?' Stephen asked, and went on to answer his own question. 'Well, you guys know my background. Being a major in the Libyan army I think in terms of simple plans that are easy to execute. On that basis I would suggest we choose between the nukes and the old ammunition ship. Knocking over those pylons should be easy, if it doesn't lead to a nuclear disaster we still black out most of the country and that alone should be good enough. Blowing up the old ship should not be too difficult although we would need a special depth charge type bomb.' He shot a glance at the Iraqi explosives man. 'You could make something up, couldn't you Alan?'

'Sure, shouldn't be a problem. What's more I'd be happy to drive the boat that dropped the charge.'

'OK, so which is it, the river or the nukes?'

For a few minutes the group remained silent as they

thought over their options. George broke the silence. 'Why not both? If we set the Thames on fire, that would draw all the emergency services down Sheerness way, then if we hit the nukes it would really create chaos. The country just wouldn't know what had hit it, or whether we would be striking again.'

The others nodded in agreement.

'OK,' George summed up. 'That's what we'll do. Now let each of us work out the detail. I would suggest a target date towards the end of August, possibly even the Bank Holiday. That gives us plenty of time. A couple of months to do all the preparation work and to plan our escape routes.'

5

1 July 202X
A Chance Meeting

A couple of weeks had passed, and Richard England received an email which would ultimately have far-reaching consequences. It was from Duckwatch:

Dear Duckwatch helper,
The officers would like to invite you to a get-together next Tuesday at the Felixstowe office. We would like to update you on the progress that we have made thanks to the help and information that we have had. We will start the meeting at 17.00 hrs and break for a meal at 19.30 hrs. If you have any special dietary requirements please let us know. The meeting can then continue on an informal basis for as long as necessary. Please let us know if you will be coming along. Thank you for your cooperation.
Yours sincerely,
Chief Inspector Jennifer Smith

Dick mused over the email, checked his diary, than made his fateful decision. He clicked on the reply button:

Thanks for the invite, will be pleased to attend. Regards, Dick England.

*   *   *

Five days later Dick drove down to the Felixstowe office. It was the back room attached to a police station that had been closed down during the cuts of the Depression years of the 2010s. He arrived just before the meeting started, found an empty seat and awaited the presentation.

Chief Inspector Jennifer Smith did the introduction. She was a handsome, well-built woman in her late forties with short-cropped fair hair.

'I would like to thank you all for coming along. My colleagues will brief you on what has been happening and how the information from your Duckwatch eyes has contributed to some successful operations. However, we will start with showing you a training film that has been made to illustrate some of the suspicious circumstances to look out for.'

The lights dimmed and the screen lit up. The show illustrated the type of incident that the Duckwatchers should be noting and reporting. One scene showed a yacht coming into a marina and people getting off dressed inappropriately for yachting. The fellows had straw boaters for hats, appropriate for a punt on the Thames but not for a North Sea passage. One of the ladies was wearing high-heeled shoes, the other had on a frilly pink calf-length dress. In another scene a large forty-foot motor cruiser tried to lie alongside a pontoon by approaching it stern first in the same manner as a car would squeeze into a parking place. The illustrations were not only nautical but applied to everyday life. There was the situation in which the paper boy went up to a house with all its curtains drawn, opened a side gate and was immediately attacked by a large dog.

When the show came to an end, Chief Inspector Smith stressed some critical points.

'You experienced sailors probably laughed at the boating scenes, but these things do sometimes crop up.

There is usually some innocent explanation, but not always. Maybe the people getting off their yacht were going to a wedding or a club ball, they might have changed on board before coming ashore. The guy trying to park his boat like a car might just have been experimenting or showing his son how not to come on to a pontoon. As for the paper boy, that one is more difficult to explain. The point is, just report all these types of observations. The SWAT team will not go charging in with guns blazing. The information will be passed on and added to other intelligence. If a picture builds up that gives rise to concern, then action will be taken. This evening we have Angela Brightone from the UK Frontier Control and Derek Catchman from the Security Services. I am not going to say which one, so we will think of him as being from CI5, more like George Cowley than Bodie or Doyle. Angela, over to you.'

Angela Brightone stood up and looked at her notes. 'I do want to thank you all for the contribution you have made,' she said. 'I would like to tell you in detail how information from Duckwatch has led to some considerable successes for the FC. However, for security reasons I have to skip the detail but I can give the overall position. A sharp-eyed yachtsman, well yachtswoman to be precise, passed on what she had seen on another yacht she had overtaken. As she approached the boat she scanned it with her binoculars and there were about a dozen adults in the cockpit and on the deck. As she drew closer they all rushed below. We added this to other reports and were able to break up a gang smuggling illegal immigrants. Another Duckwatcher was ashore scanning the sea with his high-powered glasses looking for a basking shark that had been seen in the area. He saw a yacht drop a buoy overboard, and a motor cruiser which was following behind picked it up. He could not identify the boats but again, by combining this with other information, we were able to break up a drug smuggling ring.' She paused, scanned the audience and decided that they would like another example. 'Something like the example shown in the film happened on our patch. A lady noticed that one of the houses in her lane that had recently changed occupiers had all its curtains drawn. When the snow fell she noticed that it melted on the roof, whereas the snow on the neighbouring houses remained. Even the snow on her own roof remained although she did not have loft insulation. It aroused her suspicions so she reported it. Bingo, when we raided it was found to be a cannabis factory.'

A short discussion followed, then Angela handed over to her colleague Derek Catchman.

'Hi all. I'm not quite sure where to start. I can't tell you anything about the Service or even what we do.' He paused to allow that to sink in, then continued, 'Well I suppose I can tell you that we keep a very close eye on the terrorist threat. We have many sources of information and a team of guys sorting it all out. This leads to suspicions, the suspicions lead to surveillance, and that sometimes leads to the breaking up of a gang planning to kill lots of people. What I would like to stress is that it is the little things that add up. These baddies are so smart they seldom make large noticeable errors, and it is from you guys that we get the little things. I can't give you examples like Angela did but we do need to know anything unusual. Just keep the info coming in and we'll do the rest. Maybe you see someone buying several alarm clocks. We add that info to reports of certain chemicals being stolen, and then to reports from agents abroad, and so on. It adds up and appropriate action is taken. The point I am making is that it all depends on folk like you, with your wits about you, passing on info to us. Thanks for coming. Now we will chat while we eat and even afterwards.'

With those comments the formal part of the meeting ended. Those who had been listening got up from their seats and ambled over towards the finger buffet. Richard England was amongst them. After helping himself to a few items, he absent-mindedly sat down at one of the tables, only to find, much to his surprise, that he was sitting next to the Angela Brightone who had given the talk about the Frontier Control. They started to chat about summer holidays and Dick mentioned his trip from Calais.

'Your chaps were really on the ball when we got back,' he said. '*Rosie* was only at the Roughs when one of your RIBs came up to us on a routine check. They were very polite and apologised for the intrusion but they were only doing their job – no problem as far as I was concerned. Bit of good luck as it turned out, saved us a trip into Halfpenny Pier. I was going to stop there to check in a passenger I had picked up in France, just to make sure he was legit, but your chaps took him in for me. As it turned out, it suited both of us because once he had been cleared his friends came and picked him up.'

Angela seemed intrigued by the story. 'Tell me more,' she said.

'Well I don't want to bore you with the details, nothing exciting.'

'Let me be the judge of that. What you have said is of great interest.'

'OK, but I was just trying to put in a good word for your chaps. When we were in the Canal de Calais, waiting for the lock gates in the morning, this chap came and asked if we could give him a lift to the UK. At first I thought he was one of the illegal immigrants trying to sneak into the UK. However he showed me his British passport, it had been issued in Afghanistan. He actually admitted he was from Afghanistan and had been given a British name and nationality for the work he had done for the British forces. Apparently the Taliban were after his blood. So we gave him a lift. Interesting how tight security was. I told him I would take him into Harwich for your lot to clear him; he seemed to think this was a good idea. He phoned me a couple or so weeks ago and we had lunch out. Told me how he had been cleared by the UK FC but he had to use his secret password.'

'What was that?' Angela interrupted.

'He wouldn't tell me, seems it was top secret and he could only reveal it to the entry point commander if his passport was queried.'

'That would have been me,' Angela remarked 'but it never happened. Furthermore, we didn't have longshore patrols out, well not in rubber ducks. These days they are backed by a proper vessel like a small corvette. Sounds a bit like drug smuggling. Give me your phone number would you? I may be in touch after I have checked on one or two things in the office.'

'Call me anytime.' Dick handed over his card. 'Glad to help in any way I can,' he added with a smile.

A couple of weeks later Dick received a phone call.

'Hello, England speaking.'

'Hello Mr England. We have met; my name is Derek Catchman.'

Dick thought for a few moments, then he remembered the Duckwatch meeting. 'Yes, I remember you. What can I do for you?'

'That chat you had with Angela, she followed up what you said about being intercepted at the Roughs Towers and your passenger taken ashore by the UK FC. Well she now says none of their boats were out that day and there is no record of any boat coming in for clearance of a passenger. She also does not think it was drug smuggling, as there is no word on the streets of any consignment coming in. Of course this is not for sure; it may be that drugs did come in and word has not got around, but if that is what happened it is unusual.'

Dick interrupted him. 'If it wasn't smuggling, then what was it?'

'That's the point, Mr England, we don't know, but we have some nasty suspicions. We're getting vibes from our overseas contacts that a nasty has crept in and something is being planned. We have had these scares before but they have come to nothing, so it may be this one will fizzle out – but anything you remember might help.'

'I think I told Angela all that happened, even the follow up visit when he bought me lunch. Don't think he'd do that if he was one of the bad boys.'

'What did you talk about?'

'Boats and the River Thames. Said he was going to do archaeological work up in Scotland near Inverness but he didn't say much about it. He was interested in the history of the Thames, we talked a bit about Chatham and its museum. Oh, he also asked about higher up the Thames and the Houses of Parliament which have river frontage. Come to think of it he even joked about how Guy Fawkes should have made his approach from the water, but I don't think for a moment he was serious.'

'Probably not, but an assault from the river might take the security guys by surprise. Thanks Dick, do you mind if I call you Dick?

'Sure, what'll I call you? Catchman?'

'Yes, that would be fine. If you need to contact me please do so through Angela. She has a direct secure line to this office. If this guy does contact you again, try and find out more about him – his phone number would be a great help. Thanks again.'

6

12 July 202X
Final Preparations

Two weeks following their decision meeting, the gang met up to review their progress. Again, George took the lead.

'I think it's time we reviewed our preparations. We've been here for nearly a month and we might be attracting attention, so after this meeting we will split up. We can communicate with each other by mobile phone using the coded system we devised.' The others looked a little puzzled, so he explained. 'If the locals keep seeing all of us coming and going from this place, well at first they might have accepted it, but after two months it is going to look a bit odd. I know it's not likely, but if someone complained to the police on some trivial matter, or maybe one of the locals is a Duckwatch lookout, then we could be hit. If we split up then one hit would not kill all our operations.

'Charles, you bought the place so you must stay here and Stephen you stay with him. Let the locals think you are ... well, you know what.' There were smiles all round as George continued, 'James, you and I will rent a holiday house for a month. You can use your German nationality, make out you are on holiday and it won't seem odd. Alan, that leaves you. You have the car, take the tent, and other equipment and go camping. You will be relatively comfortable. Move around every few days from site to

site. Take the RIB as well. Are you all happy with that?'
The others nodded. George continued.

'We have two plans of attack, the sunken ammunition
boat in the Thames and the nuclear power stations.
Charles have you worked out how to corrupt that diesel
fuel?'

'Yes, I don't think it will be too difficult. We know when
the tanker with the fuel is due at the site. We know where
it is coming from. We will devise some form of diversion,
get the driver away for a few minutes and then pour some
NG into the tank.'

'NG?' James asked.

'Nitro glycerine. It should mix with the diesel,' Charles
replied, looking across at the explosives expert Alan who
nodded in agreement. 'Alan says so long as we keep it cold
it will be safe. He also thinks that as it is organic it will
probably mix with the diesel and not explode until it gets
into the engine injector.'

'Where do we get the NG from?' George asked.

'No problem, Alan says he can make it here.'

Alan nodded then added, 'I will need some help if I'm
living in a tent. I need a Winchester of fuming nitric acid
and a Winchester of sulphuric and a carboy of glycerine'

'What's a Winchester, thought it was a rifle?' Stephen
asked.

'It's a large, strong, glass bottle holding about two and
a half litres. Used a lot in the chemistry labs. I can't just go
and buy them from the local chemist, they will have to be
stolen. Best we get a gang operating in another area to do
that so I'll get in touch with a contact I have who works
the Manchester area. There are chemical factories in that
part of the country. The spooks aren't daft. When it gets
reported that these chemicals have been stolen they will
start to expect a bang – but not as far away as East
Suffolk,' he added with a smile. 'Once I've made the NG

we keep it in the fridge in a thermos flask; a two pinter will be plenty'

'I'll need you guys to help,' James said. 'It'll probably need three of us to fix the tanker.'

'That'll have to be Charles and Stephen,' George interjected and saw the two nod in agreement. 'Now what about the transmission lines?'

'We do the tanker on the first Tuesday in the month. The sooner we knock over the pylons after that the better, but we must finish the job before the first Monday in the next month which is when they will test-run the diesels. The pylons will be easy. I've selected the ones. They are about five miles away from the station, out in open fields. We fix them up the night before with a delayed fuse and a small amount of explosive on their legs. If we were to blow just one leg the pylon might not fall, it could just hang by the wires. So we blow two legs at the same time and we blow them in two places about a metre and half apart. That ensures that a complete section is removed from each of the chosen legs. It will be like felling a tree; the pylon will then fall to the side that the legs were blown. It's like this,' James picked up a sheet of paper, drew a sketch of a pylon and marked off where the charges would be placed.

'Now the question is, which way do we want them to fall? There are two parallel lines, so do we topple them outwards or inwards so they crash into each other?' No one answered so he continued, 'My first thoughts were to topple them outwards but then I thought that if by some mischance they did not fall over, or if the charges on one of the pylons failed, they might survive. Therefore we will set the charges so they fall inwards towards each other and crash one line into the other. There would then be an enormous explosion as the power lines short circuit to earth, might even melt the pylon!' The others gave a bit of a snigger. 'We do four pylons, two successive pairs that are side by side.' Again he sketched the idea. 'All we need is the bangers and their timers.' He shot a glance at Stephen. 'What about your army training. Isn't this the sort of thing they taught you?'

'Sure is,' Stephen responded. 'Best things are probably what they use in the demolition industries, plastic explosives. We could simply mould some round the pylon legs and then set the timer. Want me to take care of that?' James nodded. 'OK, I've got contacts. I may be able to get some off the shelf, so to speak, but if not then they will have to be stolen – but not by us,' he added with a smile. 'Think we should call this operation Guy Fawkes?'

The others nodded in agreement except Charles. 'What happens if some hiker spots the fixings, as they will be in position a day before they go off? I know it's not likely but it could happen.'

A couple of minutes' silence followed as they all pondered the problem, then James spoke. 'It's highly unlikely a hiker would see the charges on all four pylons and even if he did he would probably take no action. But, as the problem has been raised, I have an idea to take care of the possibility. We will simply put a little note on each pylon like "Earth Leakage Assessment in progress, do not move". That should buy enough time for the big bang to occur.'

'Good we seem to have that all tied up,' George remarked. 'Now, let me tell you about the Thames job. We need to make a depth charge; Alan reckons that will not be a problem. I will find a suitable container about the size of a large bucket but one with a sealed lid. We will fill the bucket with dynamite and attach a timer with detonator. We just take the RIB out to the sunken wreck and drop our depth charge over the side. Make our way back to shore and away.

'This brings me to the matter of our getaways. Charles, you will be involved with the Guy Fawkes plot. I think it would be better if you made your escape back to Ireland. You can use your own name and passport. There are flights from a London airport. Suggest you book yourself in as soon as we have set the date. Probably the best way there would be by train and the Underground. Set up the bombs on the pylons on a Saturday night with a twenty-two-hour delay, get a morning flight on the Sunday and you'll be back in Ireland before the bang.'

Charles nodded in agreement.

'What about James and myself?' Stephen chipped in.

'No problem. James you can book the hire car until after "Events Day" – let's call it Events Day not D Day, as that might arouse suspicion. You drive down to Ramsgate on the morning of Events Day, Alan and I will meet you at the harbour after we have dropped the depth charge, probably about mid afternoon. I have arranged for our friends to have a fast motor cruiser ready and waiting in the marina. As soon as we are all present we simply slip out and head for Dunkirk. Once there we should check in but we will just stop on the visitors' pontoon, walk ashore and go our separate ways. There are no passport checks within the Continental EU. So we simply make our own way back home. Could even revert to our own names.'

'Sounds too good to be true,' James remarked.

'Yes, it does, but there are still some loose ends to tie up,' Alan reminded them. 'Where do I get the container for the depth charge from? And I will have to come here to make it up, I will also have to come here to make the NG.'

'OK,' George replied, 'but it will only need the occasional visit. We'll get the chemicals delivered here, and the plastic, one way or another. The guys that are going to steal it will be glad to get rid of it. They might talk after the event but that isn't likely as it would make them accomplices. We'll use our mobiles with our code to keep in touch. Alan, you've got the car so just go and buy the timing devices but not all from one shop. Presumably you will use an alarm clock or watch?'

'Yes, that's no problem, but what about the depth charge container?'

'Again no problem,' Charles reassured him. 'Call in at one of the building supplies places, preferably one of the large ones. Look in the paint section and pick out a commercial-sized tin of paint of some sort. Empty it out in some remote spot and there is your container.'

'OK,' was all Alan said in response.

'Finally, let us set Events Day,' George instructed as he reached for his diary. 'Bank Holiday might not be the easiest. The roads may get blocked with heavy traffic and,' he looked at Charles, 'trains might not be frequent enough to get you to London. The first Tuesday in August is the third so we need the NG by then if we are going to fix the tanker. I think we should strike soon after that just in case someone tries to test the diesels before the routine run. How about making Events Day the eighth of August?'

'I'm the one with the most homework – think I would like another week. How does the fourteenth fit?' Alan asked.

Charles consulted a set of tide tables he had bought when at Canvey Island.

'Looking at the tides, that would be better. Low water is about ten pm so if the depth charge exploded a couple of hours before then it would still create maximum blast. We could plant it at about midday which would be just after the morning low water. Absolutely ideal.'

'Yep, if we leave here towing the dinghy at about eight o'clock then we could be on the water by late morning. Where do we launch?' Alan asked George.

'Don't know yet but there must be a handy slipway in the area'

'Yes but we don't want to mess about looking for one, especially as we will have the bomb in the car.'

George thought for a few moments then had an idea. 'OK, I'll sort that out. That chap England will know somewhere. I'll contact him with some dumb story and get him to recommend a suitable launching place. Right gents, all is now settled. Let's keep in touch by phone and meet again on the twelfth of Aug, gives us one month. All agree?'

'Just one more thought,' Charles the Irishman spoke up. 'This operation Guy Fawkes, it is going to have a massive impact but it would be even more devastating if we had another Guy Fawkes as well.'

'What have you in mind?' George asked.

'Well over the other side of the country, Somerset way, there is another large nuclear power station with three reactors. If the pylons carrying that electricity could be disabled it would double the grid problem. I have got some contacts in that part of the country who might well be looking for a job to further our cause. How about if I have a word with them?'

George looked round at the others but no one spoke so he broke the silence. 'Involving others weakens our security, how secure are your contacts? Can they be trusted, are they under surveillance? Is it worth the risk?'

'They're good guys. They belong to the same organisation as myself and I know they are over here as sleepers. I don't think we need to worry about the security angle. I would just suggest that they knocked over a couple of pylons on the fourteenth of August and leave the rest to them.'

'OK,' George said, 'let's put it to the vote. What do you say chaps?'

One by one they all gave a thumbs-up. George continued, 'Over to you, Charles. Don't tell them about Guy Fawkes, just suggest it would be helpful if they did the pylon job at the time we specify.'

7

Richard England was about to shut the front door of his bungalow when the phone rang. For a moment he hesitated, then decided to delay his start and answer the call.

'Dick England, who's calling?'

'Mr England? This is George Monarch, how are you?'

'Still alive. And you? How are things in Scotland?' Dick was remembering his brief to find out as much as he could about the mysterious Mr Monarch.

'Oh, OK.'

'Whereabouts are you working?'

The question took the terrorist by surprise but he had done some homework and responded, 'At Culloden, it is near Inverness. Some big battle was fought there a long time ago.'

'Yes, I did learn about that when I was at school.' Dick replied, trying to keep the conversation going and not admitting he had visited the old battleground some years ago, 'but I thought that battle field had already been fully explored?'

'We are working just near it,' George responded, then changed his line of chat. 'I only wanted to ask you for a bit more information. My friend here has a theory that there is some treasure or something archaeological that has not yet been discovered near the entrance to the River Thames. You told me about a place called Chatham where there was an old ship-building yard?'

He paused for breath and Dick interrupted. 'Yes, that is up the Medway.'

'It isn't the boat yard that interests my friend, it's one of the sand banks off the coast. I think he mentioned the name Sheerness, does that mean anything?'

'Sheerness is at the mouth of the Medway. I did explain that when we chatted over lunch.' Dick's mind was not on the conversation; he was wondering how he could get more out of the caller. Then he had an idea. 'Was it about Medway off the Thames that you were calling?'

'Yes, I think it is probably the Thames near this place called Sheerness.'

Now Dick decided on a gamble. 'OK George, but I need to get my old charts out. I don't want to give you the wrong information. Tell you what, give me your phone number and I'll call back in a few minutes when I've got the charts.'

George was bewildered, and he did not want to give his phone number. 'That's OK, Mr England, I will hold on while you look. I am on a mobile and it would be expensive for you to call me back.'

Dick thought fast. 'No, I will have to ring off, I'm afraid. I am expecting an urgent call any minute now and I don't want the phone line blocked while I look out the charts. It might take longer than I thought. I don't mind the cost of calling you back.'

The terrorist realised he was cornered. If he terminated the conversation then suspicions would be aroused. England's request was quite reasonable and if he did not comply that would look odd, so he decided to play along and gave Dick his mobile phone number.

Dick waited ten minutes before he phoned back.

'Hello George, sorry for the delay but that phone call I was waiting for did come in just after you rang off.' To give realism he added, 'It was from a friend in Holland; his wife has been very ill. He called to tell me she is now in hospital and he was on his way to see her. Now how can I help you?'

'Well, Mr England, my friend has a small towable motor boat, it is about six metres long and has a little cabin. We have a week's holiday in August and he wants to come and explore and see if he can find anything to support his ideas. He lives in the Birmingham area of England and has his boat there so he thought we could drive down towing the boat and spend a few days exploring.'

'Seems a good idea, how can I help?'

'He is interested in the sand banks off a place called Shoeburyness; mentioned something like Spile and Middle Sand?'

Dick scanned the Thames chart and noted the areas that had been mentioned; so far it all seemed reasonable.

'Yes, I see them on the chart. What about them?'

'We will need somewhere we can launch from and I wondered if there is anywhere you would recommend?'

Dick looked at the chart again. He was puzzled. He could not understand how someone who must have looked at a marine chart and understood the markings could not work out for themselves the best place for launching a small boat. Nevertheless he decided to play along.

'For Middle Sand you would probably be better launching from Whitstable. I know there is a good sailing club there but I doubt if they would want casual visitors using their slipway. The place where I moor up when I am in those parts is Dutchville, so named because a few hundred years ago the Dutch tried to capture the village. They failed but the name stuck. However that might be too far from where you want to be, about ten miles from the Middle Sands but about eight from the Spile. What's your friend's boat like, does it have a large engine?'

'I don't know about the engine but he did say it could do about fifteen knots, whatever they are'.

Dick smiled to himself at the fellow's ignorance of nautical distances. 'Knots are nautical miles, so if the boat will do fifteen knots then it would take only between half and an hour to get from from Dutchville to the sands. That should be OK.'

'Thank you, but is there a place to launch from at this Dutchville?'

'Yes, no problems. Just follow the signs for BBBY, that stands for Bill Brontwich Boat Yard. You will come to a pole barrier which says "Private, no public access". Lift the barrier, and drive in until you come to a small office cum chandlery. Call in there, pay your dues. I don't know what he charges but it won't be much, and then you'll get the OK to launch. It's a fairly long slipway but you can back the car down it so no problems.'

'Thank you, Mr England, that sounds as if it will suit us. I must get back to work now.'

'Glad to have been helpful. Have a good holiday, hope you find the treasure, must say bye for now.'

With that, Dick put the phone down. He had what he wanted and wasted no time in calling Chief Inspector Jennifer Smith at Duckwatch. He briefed her on the conversation and gave her the phone number that Richard Monarch had used. Jennifer also wasted no time as she passed the information to Derek Catchman from the Security Service.

Dick collected his thoughts. He had intended to go down to *Rosie* and check her over, run up her engines and then return home. The days had long passed when he was able to sail the boat single-handed so, unless a crew was available, he had to be content with a visit, relaxing with a cup of tea, then returning without slipping the mooring. Talk of the Thames and the Medway had aroused his thoughts of past trips – maybe he and *Rosie* could satisfy their nostalgia if Rodney was free. He picked up the phone again and dialled.

'Hello Dick.' Rodney MacDonald answered even before Dick had spoken. 'How's things?'

Dick ignored the question. 'Rod. I was wondering if you had any free time. I would just love to get another trip in before old age disables me? I've been thinking about the trip we did back in 2000 when we went up the Thames to St Cath's. Thought maybe we could dawdle down there and visit the Blackwater on our way. I'd love to go back to Brightlingsea again.'

A short silence followed then Rodney replied, 'I'm a bit pushed at the moment and the weather forecast is not too inviting for the next week or so. I don't like that big depression out in the Atlantic. Reckon I could be free at the end of the first week in August. How about pencilling in the seventh for starting?'

Dick's pulse started to race at the thought of this last trip.

'That would be great. I'll get *Rosie* ready so we can make a prompt getaway, weather permitting that is.'

'OK Blighty, I'll put it in my diary. No promises but should be all right, I'll keep you posted. By the way, don't forget that bottle of malt you promised.'

'I won't. Cheers, see you in August if not before.'

It was 10 days later when Dick England got a call from Catchman.

'Mr England, how are you? We've been following up the leads you gave. That call you received did not come from Scotland, more like East Anglia. Also there is no record of any archaeological work currently being undertaken near the Culloden site, so clearly something is wrong. Our chaps have been able to monitor some of the phone calls from that number you gave us. On the face of things they sound quite innocent.'

'How do you mean?'

'Well the conversations would be more appropriate to a set of actors or a concert party. They talk about meeting on a desert island; names like George Formby and Charlie Chaplin, keep cropping up.'

'Any other names?'

'Yes, I was only pausing for breath; there has also been mention of Alan Banks who was the star of an old TV series, some sort of detective I believe. Then there is Simon Templar, The Saint of course, and finally John Steed from the Avengers. Could well be that they are just an entertainment group imitating these characters, but that would not tie up with all the lies about being in Scotland and involving this chap who claimed to be from Afghanistan. We are still checking on that story, doesn't ring true. Can't find any record, but security is very tight, even to us, when new identities are awarded.'

'Sounds dodgy to me,' Dick commented.

'It sure does but there is something else. They talk about what looks like some sort of event or operation. It could be the name of a show or something but it just doesn't seem right. They talk about Guy Fawkes, not the chap himself or what he actually did but as if it was going to be some sort of happening. It could well be a show they are putting on on the fifth of November but it didn't quite gel to that. I suppose you've no suggestions?'

Dick thought for a moment then said, 'It might seem a bit far-fetched but when I was talking to that chap George Monarch, the one who said he came from Afghanistan, he jokingly suggested that Guy Fawkes could have done a better job if he had attacked from the Thames. If he is in with terrorists, maybe they are planning to attack Parliament from the river? If they got in that way and massacred a few hundred MPs or Lords that would certainly be a big hit.'

'It does sound a bit far-fetched, but Mr England I think you could be right. If we knew when they would strike we could be ready for them. Any suggestions?'

'The chap said he and his friend had a holiday in August and he wanted me to suggest a place where he could launch his boat.'

'What sort of boat?'

'About a twenty-footer with a small cabin. It must be light as he said they would trail it by car, also it could do fifteen knots. I suggested Bill Brontwich's Boat Yard at Dutchville. That's about forty miles from Westminster but even at ten knots they could do it in the morning. On the other hand, surely it would be much better to launch somewhere else.'

'Yes there must be other places nearer. Anyhow Parliament would not be in session in August, so there'd be no MPs to massacre. On the other hand, because it was not in session, security would be that much less. Well thanks for your help.'

'You're welcome.'

'Hang on, there's something else. The other phrases that cropped up a few times were Clifton James and CJ, which we assume referred to Clifton James.'

'The actor?'

'Well probably. He appeared in one or more of the Bond films. I suppose it would fit in with the other characters like Templar and Steed in the group. If you have any thoughts let me know.'

'Wilco,' replied Dick using an old VHF proword. Then he added, 'By the way I'm likely to be cruising in August.

I'm pencilled in to start on the seventh, probably get back here about a week later. I do have a mobile on the boat, don't use it ashore. Well when you are in your eighties you don't keep up with all this new technology. I'll give Angela Brightone the number before we leave just in case you want to contact me again.'

'Thank you very much Mr England, your cooperation is much appreciated. I think I ought to give you my direct line number just in case you remember something that is urgent. Got a pencil?'

As Dick put the phone down he tugged gently at the lobe of his ear as he thought the matter over, before resuming what he had been doing before the call.

8

It was a pleasant evening on 3 August. The terrorists had worked out their plan, now they were about to put it into practice. About a couple of miles from Deephole there was a lay-by on the road the fuel tanker would be using. The plotters were in a car at the far end of the lay-by waiting for the signal from George who was stationed a mile further back. Charles and Stephen were dressed in police uniforms that they had hired from a theatrical props agency. James was dressed in dark brown overalls, and carried a clip board and a torch. They had waited nearly half an hour when their hand-held radio came to life.

'The ship has just passed,' was all George reported.

James reached into the car, took out a sign that lit up with the word POLICE and placed it on the roof of the car. As the fuel tanker approached, Charles, with Stephen at his side, stepped out into the road and in the fading light waved the tanker to stop in the lay-by.

'What's the problem officer?' the driver asked as he leaned out of the cab window.

'Sorry to stop you sir,' Charles replied. 'You are on your way to Deephole Nuclear Station I presume?'

'Yes officer, is there something wrong?'

'I hope not sir but,' he hesitated for effect then continued, 'we've been asked to check your vehicle over before it gets to the site. The security boys have got the idea that the site might be targeted and we've been asked to make sure that no one has done anything nasty to your vehicle. You've got a lot of fuel there and if it blew up on the site ... well need I say more? I've already said too much. So we would like to carry out a quick check under and over the vehicle.'

'I've not heard anything about this. Why not make the check when I get to site?'

'I don't really know sir, we are just following orders. It won't take long.'

'All right, if you must. Get on with it but you won't find anything. The vehicle hasn't been out of my sight.'

James appeared from the background with a clipboard in his hand and a flask of ice-cold NG tucked inside his overall. First he looked under the vehicle and around the outside.

'All clear there boss,' he said to Charles. 'I'll just check over the top. Tell the driver I will need to take a look inside through the inspection port. If it is locked ask for the key.'

'Did you hear that?' Charles said to the driver. 'No problems so far but he wants to peep into the tank. Please give me the key to the inspection port.'

The driver handed over the key. James climbed up the ladder on the rear of the tank and then onto the top of the vehicle. He opened the inspection port, took out the flask from under his overall and gently poured the NG into the fuel. He closed and locked the port, tucked the flask back where it had come from and as he started to climb down called out, 'It's all clear here boss. Reckon it must have been a false alarm. OK to let the chap get on his way.'

Charles gave the driver the thumbs-up, James handed back the keys, and both stepped to one side and waved the vehicle on.

Once the tanker was out of sight they removed the

police sign, got into the car, drove to pick up George from his look-out position and returned to the chapel.

As the fuel tanker approached the nuclear power station, the gate keeper opened the first of the two gates allowing the vehicle to enter the cage. He carried a small black box the size of a mobile phone and handed it to the driver.

'Sign in please,' was all he said. The driver pressed some buttons and a green light came on as he handed the security check back to the gate keeper who then remarked, 'You're a bit on the late side tonight.'

'Well it's not my fault; that security check held me up. Still, I got here before the deadline.'

'What check?'

The driver explained how the police had stopped him and how they had carried out the inspection.

'That's odd. If they had got wind of something I would have thought we'd have been put on alert. You stay here for a bit while I make some enquiries. You said two of the guys were in police uniform, did you get their numbers?'

'Well no, it was getting dark, I didn't even get out of the cab. I suppose I should have asked for some ID but they didn't hijack me so I don't see why they would stop me if it weren't on the level.'

'Maybe, but I'm going to make some checks.' He went inside his gatehouse and phoned the local police HQ. They knew nothing about the stop and search. He phoned the Head of Site Security who told him to impound the vehicle and not to let it onto site. It would be dealt with in the morning.

The investigation that followed finally found traces of NG in the fuel. It was not publicised but security at the station was put on alert.

*   *   *

Back at the chapel the quartet congratulated themselves on the success of their mission. Everything had gone according to plan. The tanker was one of the older designs with filling hatches on top of the tank. Had it been more modern these would not have been there, in which case the plan would have failed. Now all they had to do was to put the finishing touch to their operations on the fourteenth.

Dick 'Blighty' England and Rodney MacDonald boarded *Rose of England* on the 10th of August and set off on what was planned to be Dick's last cruise before he put his beloved boat up for sale. Age was catching up with him. Rodney was not such an enthusiast but was doing the trip with Dick for old times' sake. The weather was set fine, something unusual for an English summer, and they intended to make the most of it.

In calm seas they slipped out of the Deben, called in at Brightlingsea for a 24-hour stop over, spent another day on the river Blackwater getting up to Maldon and back before picking up a mooring in Bradwell Creek. It was there that Dick's mobile phone demanded his attention.

'This is the cruise ship *Rose of England*, Master speaking,' he said with a mischievous sense of humour.

'I hope I haven't called the wrong number, is there a Mr England on board?'

'Yes, this is England speaking, how can I help?'

'Oh Dick, I didn't recognise your voice. Don't want to interrupt your holiday but thought I ought to put you in the picture. This is Catchman, if you hadn't guessed.'

'I thought it might be, after you started to chat. What can I do for you? I haven't had any more contact with our mysterious Mr Monarch.'

'Well something has happened but I'm not sure whether it is tied in with him. Also we are picking up more phone intelligence.'

'Go on.'

'There was an attempt to sabotage the diesel generators at Deephole power station. Some bogus police stopped the fuel delivery tanker and spiked its load with nitro glycerine. Fortunately the security people at the station were on the ball and grew suspicious of the tanker driver's experience, carried out an investigation and found the nasty. I wondered if your Mr Monarch had ever asked for info about Deephole?'

'No, never mentioned it. Anything else?'

'They still talk about Clifton James and we can't see any connection. Incidentally we are keeping a look out for a twenty-foot small cabin boat being towed along the roads in the Thames area. We can't stop every car towing a boat, but let me know if you see anything suspicious.'

'OK. Good luck, or should I say good hunting?'

9

13 August 202X
Finale

Dick and Rodney waited for the start of the flood tide before *Rose of England* slipped her mooring in Bradwell creek. They made their way past the remains of the old nuclear power station and then out of the river Blackwater. Their course took them down Barrow Deep, amongst the newly constructed wind farms, into the Warp then the Medway channel. In the late afternoon they picked up a mooring for the night at Dutchville.

At the chapel, the conspirators were putting the final touch to their plans for the evening and the coming day. It was mid afternoon and James was briefing the others.

'It will take four of us to fix the pylons, Alan, Charles and Stephen you have drawn the short straws to come with me. We split into two groups. Alan and Charles you two go together. Stephen, you come with me. We will take a pair of binoculars with us. We shouldn't need them but if by any chance we get challenged as to why we are walking across the field, use the excuse that you are bird watching and thought you saw an owl.

'We will go in the same car, I will navigate, Charles you drive. We go out of here and head for Deephole going through Munchington. About a mile the other side there is an unmade track leading into a large field. I think it might be a relic of an old World War Two airfield. About two hundred metres down the track we come to a line of pylons. Alan and Charles, you will tackle the nearest. Stephen and myself will drive back out of the track onto the road. It doubles back on itself for a short distance and in doing so passes the next pair of pylons. We will then go and deal with them before returning to pick up Alan and Charles. The lines pass over a couple of cottages just before they cross the road. There is a chance that when the pylons blow the lines will collapse onto the cottages and also onto the road.'

He paused, took a sip of orange juice, then continued.

'Each pair of us will take eight charges, two timers and two batteries. On the inside of our selected pylons two separate charges will be placed, one on each of the inside legs. On these legs the charges should be placed about a metre and a half apart. The idea is that when they explode a complete section of steel will be blown out, effectively removing the legs from one side of the pylon so causing it to topple.'

'Why do two pylons? If one toppled wouldn't it crash into the other one?' Stephen asked.

'Yes, it probably would but I can't be sure, so we'll do both in the pair. It will take only a few more minutes.' He grinned as he spoke and the others nodded.

'OK,' Stephen conceded and James continued

'Tape the charges in position, then connect all four on the pylon in parallel to the timer and the battery. You must set the timer before making the final connection to the battery. Finally, tie this tag on the pylon at about eye level. It says "Do not remove these wires. Earth leakage measurement in progress". When Stephen and I have fixed our target we will drive back and collect you. Don't forget, if you meet anyone, you are looking for the owl. If you are interrupted while fixing the charge, which is highly unlikely, explain you are from British Grid and measuring the earth leakage. Say that the alternating current induces a fluctuating magnetic field and this causes a small current to drain to earth through the pylon. If need be, add that your package is measuring the magnetic flux at the base of the pylon. If pressed further, which is unlikely, make out you can't say more for security reasons.'

James looked round at the others then resumed. 'Oh yes, cover the battery and timer with a few clumps of earth so they are not likely to be seen. No one will go close to the pylon but we don't want the bangers seen from the road. The timers are set to trigger twenty-two hours after connecting. Make the connection at exactly 23.00 hours which means they will blow at nine pm the next day, by which time we will be well away.'

'Better synchronise our watches.' Stephen suggested.

After they had done so Alan asked, 'What time are our friends in the West Country going to make their play?'

'10 minutes after we blow but it is not critical.'

'My turn next.' George took up the plotting. 'Alan and I plan to leave here about six in the morning, so we won't have all that much sleep after the pylon caper. We will take the RIB and also Alan's depth charge. It is time triggered and we will set it before we leave to explode at seven pm.'

'Why don't you set it when you get down there? Is there an anti-handling trigger on it?' Stephen asked.

'Yes, there is. Once we have sealed down the lid it can't be opened again. Setting it and sealing it is no simple task and it is best done here. It also means that if anyone stops us and takes the charge away it will go off when they try to take a look inside.' George paused while the others smiled. 'We should make Dutchville and BBBY, that's the boat yard where we plan to launch, by mid morning. That will be about half tide which will make the launching of the RIB fairly easy. We will ditch the charge late morning then scarper back ashore, abandon the RIB and drive down to Ramsgate to meet up with you guys. We then start our trip to the Continent. Oh, by the way, the cruiser you will be looking for will probably be on the Visitors' Berth. It will be flying a Belgian flag and the name is *Fleur de Veurne*. Any questions?'

'Yes, what's the colour of this boat?' Stephen asked.

'Blue hull with white superstructure.' George paused for a moment. 'Charles, you got your air ticket booked?'

'Sure have. Leaves London 13.00 hours so I should be well clear when the fireworks start.'

That evening the quartet went out and set their charges just as they had planned. Alan and Charles fixed theirs then started to make their way back down the unmade track towards the road. A man walking his dog passed them and spoke. 'Great evening, ain't it?'

'Sure is,' Charles replied. 'Have you seen the owl? Told there was one about but no sign of it. Still, enjoyed the walk.' He patted the dog and walked on.

Stephen and James had parked at the side of the road and gone through a gap in the hedge. Several cars passed but none stopped. No one accosted them so they did not have to use their prepared speech.

The next morning the conspirators broke up. The Irishman made his way to London and James drove Stephen to Ramsgate, arriving about midday. They left the car in the short-term car park near the marina and weren't bothered if it got wheel clamped for overstaying its time. They found *Fleur de Veurne*, introduced themselves to the skipper, went below and kept a low profile.

George and Alan kept to their plan. They hitched the RIB up to the car, stowed the home-made depth charge in the boot and left just before 7 am. There was a lot of traffic about which slowed them down a little and they reached the Queen Elizabeth Bridge two and a quarter hours later. Most of the vehicles approaching the control cubicles had season passes and were able to drive straight through, but the terrorists with their boat in tow had to go through the manned control point. They paid their toll and as they started to drive off a policeman flagged them down.

'Good morning sir, just a routine check. When were your tyres last changed?'

'I'm not sure, officer,' Alan replied, trying hard not to show his anxiety. 'I leave that sort of thing to my garage.'

'A lot of motorists do but tyres wear between garage inspections. By the way, which garage do you use?'

Alan though fast, then remembered the garage local to the chapel.

'Bloggs & Co, it's one of those odd little garages out in the wilds of Suffolk,' he replied, trying a touch of humour, but the police officer did not seem very interested. Another policeman had joined him.

'Check the tyres, Smith,' the first officer instructed.

'Yes, Guv.' The officer went down on his knees as if to check the tyres, but in fact had a good look under the car. Meanwhile the first officer continued to talk to Alan.

'I see you've a boat with you. On holiday?'

'Yes, officer, thought we'd have a few days' fishing.'

'Where were you heading for?'

Alan's mind was racing, wondering what to say, when George interrupted. He had been puzzled as to why the second policeman had called the other one Guv. Normal rankers would have said Sarge, or even a first name. The use of the word Guv indicated that this was no ordinary stop and check, more like the security forces at work. On that basis he thought an element of truth might pay off.

'We were hoping to meet up with a friend who has a motor cruiser, a chap called Richard England. Don't know him very well, but I did crew for him once on a Channel passage.'

'So what's the name of his boat?'

'*Rose of England.*'

'And where are you meeting?'

'Well we haven't made any firm arrangements, we just mentioned that we fancied a bit of sea fishing and he suggested the Medway or Swale area and told us to look out for him'

'Can I see your fishing gear? Open the boot, please,' the policeman demanded.

Alan remained calm as he got out of the car and walked round to the boot. George put his hand in his pocket and grasped a small revolver. He did not want to have to use it but, if necessary, he would do so. Alan opened the boot. Before they had left the chapel he had put some fishing gear in there and was reasonably happy it would pass inspection, but the depth charge would not. The officer looked over the rods and nets then noticed the metal container.

'What's in there? Looks rather large for bait,' he said. Alan and Stephen had made the bomb from a large commercial tin of wood preservative. It still had its original markings. Alan was able to continue the bluff.

'It's anti-woodworm stuff. Bought it at a boot sale on our way down here. Got a use for it when we get back.'

The officer wandered over to his colleague to chat. It was a deliberate ploy. If the car they had stopped was legitimate it would just remain and wait for the all clear, but if they were the terrorists they were looking for, then they would probably make a dash for it and end up being caught by another team a little further down the road.

The first officer conferred quietly, 'Looks a bit odd. Couldn't see anything underneath. We were briefed to be on the lookout for a car towing a twenty-foot boat with a small cabin. That inflatable isn't anything like it. It would be a long trip up the river from the Medway to Westminster in that little thing. We'll just log it down and let them go.' With that he walked back to the car.

'Sorry to have delayed you sir, just one of those routine checks we get lumbered with from time to time. Enjoy your fishing.'

'Thank you, officer,' Alan replied. He started the engine and drove off.

'That was a close call,' George remarked. 'Wouldn't be surprised if they have got onto our plot but they will be too late.'

Alan agreed. They were on their way. The remaining part of the journey was uneventful.

It had just turned 7 am when farmer Ralph Jones's phone rang. He was about to start his breakfast but he put aside his dish of cornflakes, got up and answered.

'R J Farms, who's speaking?'

Much to his surprise it was his golfing friend.

'Morning Ralph, Derek here. Thought I would give you a call. I was driving past your field on the Munchington Road last evening, just by where the power lines cross. A car was parked by the gap in the hedge and a couple of chaps got out and went into the field. I didn't stop, at the time I thought maybe they were going for a pee. Maybe they were, but in view of the police warning about an illegal rave being set up somewhere I thought you ought to know. Probably nothing but it might be worth checking out.'

'Thanks Derek. As you say, it was probably quite innocent but I will drive over after breakfast and check it out. I suppose you didn't get the car details?'

'Well no, it was only when I got home I began to wonder so decided to give you a call now. Oh, come to think of it, the car was a black saloon, but that's all I recall.'

'Thanks again, just can't be too careful these days. I will check it out.' As he put the phone down, Ralph's mind was mulling over the possibilities. He decided to finish his breakfast before getting the Range Rover out and driving over to the field.

He parked at the place where Stephen and James had been, got out and entered his field but saw nothing unusual. He was about to leave when he noticed what looked like a track through the wheat which was awaiting its turn for the harvester. He followed it to the nearest pylon where he saw the devices the terrorists had left. His body tensed, his heart raced, then he saw the little ticket tied to the metalwork. When he read it he relaxed and, accepting it had been a false alarm, made his way to the car and drove back to the farm.

He was having his lunch when he had second thoughts about the little notices he had seen attached to the pylons. It puzzled him why they would have been fixed in the late evening and why British Grid had not given him prior notice as they usually did when they had maintenance work to do. He decided to follow it up. He looked out his correspondence file and found a letter, about two years old, from British Grid. It had a phone number for enquiries. He decided to follow it up.

A recorded voice spoke to him. 'Thank you for calling the British Grid. This call may be recorded for training purposes. Please choose from the following options. If you are calling about your gas supply press one...' Ralph waited impatiently as the voice droned on giving him option after option. Finally he chose the one for complaints and pressed button eight. Then he got the voice again: 'Thank you for calling the Complaints Division. All our operators are busy, your call is number three in a queue. Please wait, your call is important to us.'

After six minutes, just as he was about to put the phone

down in disgust, the music stopped and a voice came on line.

'I apologise for keeping you waiting, how can I help?'

'It's a question of me helping you ...'

The voice interrupted him. 'Your name, and for security reasons can I have your date of birth?'

Ralph was beginning to lose patience but controlled his emotions and replied, 'Ralph Jones, 13 June 1962.'

'Thank you Mr Jones, what is the nature of your complaint?'

'I haven't got a complaint but I want to pass on what could be a vital piece of information to you. I farm a field alongside the B9876 about a mile from the town of Munchington in Suffolk. A line of pylons, carrying power from the Deephole nuclear power station are in my field.' He paused to collect his thoughts.

The voice cut in, 'Is there a problem over the wayleave payment?'

'No, please just listen. A friend reported seeing a suspicious car parked at the entrance to the field last night. I went to have a look this morning and on a pair of the pylons there were a couple of small packages with wires coming out of them into the ground. There was also a note saying "Earth Leakage Test in progress leave in place" or words to that effect. I just wanted to alert you to this to be sure that it is legitimate. We've been worried for some time that terrorists might try and blow up a pylon. They do carry an enormous amount of electricity.'

'Thank you for telling us, Mr Jones, I will pass it on to the Maintenance and the Research Divisions. I expect they will contact you in the morning. Do you have an email address?'

'Yes.' Ralph gave the voice his email address.

'Thank you Mr Jones, do check your emails, especially in the morning. I will pass on your information to the other departments by email so I expect they will contact you that way.'

'Can't something be done sooner? This could spell disaster.'

'I am not doubting you, and we will check it out, but it is very likely it will be genuine. I do know that there has been some concern with power loss from the transmission lines so it is probably the research scientists making measurements. If they were bombs they would have gone off by now. It is most likely a hoax. Thank you for calling.' With that the phone line went dead.

As Ralph put the phone down he muttered to himself, 'Well at least I tried.'

When George and Alan reached the outskirts of Dutchville they stopped and asked directions for Brontwich's boat yard. Shortly afterwards they saw the sign and arrow to BBBY. The yard was surrounded by a six-foot security fence and a double gate at the road entrance. Alan stopped the car, got out and walked over to the old shipping container which served as the yard's office. He was greeted by Joan Brontwich, a young girl in her late teens.

'Can I help?'

'Could we launch our RIB from your slipway? Our friend Richard England who sometimes cruises this way said you would probably allow us to launch. Of course, we are quite happy to pay. Just want a day's fishing, rod and line stuff, in salt water.'

'Yes, my dad charges twenty quid a day for casuals.' She remembered her father had briefed her about the call he had received from the police to be aware that some terrorists could want to launch a boat. He had said they were looking out for a twenty-footer with a small cabin. Joan could see out of the open door that this was nothing like that, so she took the proffered £20 note.

'I keep the gate locked, lots of thieving going on these days, not like when my granddad started the business. I can let you through from here.' She pointed to a switch on the desk in front of her, then continued, 'Take this disc and when you want to leave slip it into that box by the side of the gate. You can then open the gate but make sure you close it afterwards.'

'Oh, that will be fine,' Alan confirmed. Then he asked, just for completeness, 'Would we be able to leave the RIB here for a few days? If the fishing is good we would probably like to come back.'

'I'll have to ask Dad about that, the yard gets pretty full this time of year.'

'In that case, don't bother,' Alan snapped back; he did not want any delays and had seen the girl edge towards the phone. There was something about his attitude that didn't seem quite right to Joan. It might have been his Eastern European accent or that he was not dressed as she would have expected for a genuine fisherman. She remembered that the police were after a boat with a small cabin, but what if they had got it wrong? She decided to call her dad before letting them in.

'Dad did ask me to let him know about visitors, we get so many dubious customers here. Of course you aren't, but I'll just give him a shout before I let you in.' As she took a step towards the door she met George who had become impatient waiting in the car and decided to come and investigate.

'Don't let her out,' Alan called out. 'I think she's sussed us.' George pushed the girl back into the office. His companion took a flick knife from his pocket and stabbed the girl in the throat. She coughed, spluttered blood, and died.

'That's the switch for the barrier,' Alan said to his partner. 'Open the bloody thing and let's get down to the slip before anyone else arrives.'

George did just that and the two then rushed back to the car and followed the track to the slipway. The barrier remained open. He reversed the car towards the water, stopped when the trailer was just a few feet away and with George started to unload the car, including the depth charge, into the RIB.

Richard Harry England and Rodney MacDonald were sitting on the afterdeck of *Rose of England* enjoying a mid morning cuppa and biscuit.

'Were you thinking of moving out today Blighty, or having a lazy day? If you want to make Saint Cath's marina we ought to be leaving, the tide is now on the flood.'

Dick remained silent, staring into space.

'Blighty, I said are we going or staying?'

'Sorry,' Dick responded, shaking his head. 'My mind was miles away, well not literally miles. I was thinking – trying to remember an old film I'd seen many years ago, probably as long ago as the sixties. Don't know why I should remember it now; strange how we get these thoughts come to the fore for no apparent reason. It was about how the Germans were deceived during the war.'

'You mean "The Man Who Never Was"? The secret service got hold of a dead body, dressed it as an officer in one of the services and launched it from a submarine near the Spanish coast. It carried false papers about some proposed landings. The Jerry agent there got wind of it, managed to get a shufti at the papers, reported back to his masters and the Germans were fooled into thinking the Allies were not going to invade where they actually did. Somewhere in the Med campaign I think.'

'No, it wasn't that one. I'm thinking about an actor getting dressed up as a general and parading around the Med area to make the Germans think D Day was being planned for that part of the world.'

'You mean "I was Monty's Double"?'

'Yes. It's coming back now. That was the story; the chap who played Monty in the film was the same actor who had really been Monty's double. Can't remember his name, can you?'

'Yes, it was a chap called M.E. Clifton James. Don't know why he always had the M.E. tag, maybe to distinguish him from another Clifton James. It ends with the Germans being so fooled they even try to kidnap him but John Mills comes to the rescue at the last minute. Good film.'

'Clifton James! By God, that's it!'

'That's what?'

'The code word. That chap from security, he said they had intercepted the words CJ or Clifton James being used by the suspects on their phones. It must have been code for Montgomery, not Monty the General but the ship the *Richard Montgomery*. That explains why that chap, the one we picked up at Calais calling himself George Monarch, has been asking me about the *Richard Montgomery* and where to launch a boat from at Dutchville. He was talking about a twenty-footer with a small cabin but you wouldn't need that to trigger the *Montgomery*, just a small explosive charge and a dinghy – a RIB like the one that was used to meet us off the Roughs. I bet those bastards are out to explode the *Montgomery*.'

'Dick, you could be right! Where did you suggest they launched from?'

'Bill Brontwich's yard.'

'Well that's just over there,' Rodney remarked, pointing to a slipway running out into the mud a mere few hundred yards away. England's mind raced, then he came to a decision and spoke.

'Rod, I'm going to take our dinghy and go ashore. I'll have a word with Bill at the yard and tell him to look out for a couple of chaps who want to launch a RIB. If there are any and they mention my name, delay them. Think of a pretext and call the police.' He reached inside the afterdeck locker, took out a sheath knife still in its sheath and tucked it into the back of his shorts.

'Careful with that Blighty, you could get arrested for having an offensive weapon on you in a public place.'

'Sod that, I used to wear it when I was in the Boy Scouts, it was part of our optional uniform. Anyway I have a good excuse: if challenged I will claim I need to carry a knife in case the prop on the outboard gets fouled with weed or rope. You can support me by pointing out it has happened before. Remember the time we were in Butley Creek and the outboard motor prop picked up a piece of fishing net? Had to cut it free then.' With that he pulled their dinghy to the side of *Rose of England* and stepped into it. Meanwhile Rodney had picked up the binoculars and was scanning the shore. Dick was about to pull the starting cord on the engine when Rodney spoke up.

'Hold it. You won't believe this but there is a car backing down the slip pushing a RIB. Could be your friends have arrived, or maybe it's just some guys going fishing.'

Dick thought fast. 'Inside my cabin there is a notebook on the starboard shelf. You'll see a phone number against the name Catchman. Ring that number and tell him what's happened. Ask for Derek Catchman, he's some sort of secret service chap.'

With that Dick pulled the starting cord, the engine fired up and he cast off, heading for the shore and the launching ramp. Rodney put down the binoculars, went down below into Dick's cabin, found the note book and the telephone number. He picked up his mobile and called the mysterious Catchman.

The call was successful, he briefed the man and returned on deck just in time to see his friend arrive at the slipway. Through the binoculars he could see what happened next.

Dick ran the dinghy up alongside the slipway and walked across to the RIB which was now detached from the car and ready for launching. One chap was holding the boat but looking the other way, the second one was at the car.

'Going fishin'? Dick asked as he reached the RIB.

'Yes,' came the reply, and in that instant Dick realised his worst fears were well founded. The voice was that of the man who had pleaded for the lift to England from Calais, the man who called himself George Monarch. As Dick made his decision the fellow looked up and recognised Dick.

'Mr England! Yes we've changed our minds my fr...' His voice tailed off. Dick had reached for his sheath knife and took a step towards the RIB. As he moved with knife in hand the terrorist reached into his pocket and took out the revolver. Dick took one more step forward and plunged the knife into the sponson of the RIB. The air hissed as it escaped and the sponson collapsed just as the terrorist squeezed the trigger of his revolver. The bullet hit Dick square in the chest. He fell slumped across the RIB.

Monarch rushed up to the car where Alan sat behind the wheel.

'Quick, get out of here, that chap England turned up. He must have guessed what we were up to; he sabotaged the boat. We can't get to the *Montgomery* now. I had to shoot him. Move before the police arrive. Ramsgate, here we come.'

The trailer had already been unhitched so Alan started the engine, drove to the gate which was still open and went through. As he did so Bill Brontwitch came out of a nearby shed and shouted, 'What the hell is going on?'

'Forgot something, back soon,' Alan shouted as he hit the accelerator.

Bill ran over to the office to find his daughter lying dead in a pool of her own blood.

An hour later the terrorists were in Ramsgate and aboard the *Fleur de Veurne*. The boat quickly slipped its berth and headed for Dunkirk, taking its passengers to freedom.

On board *Rose of England* Rodney, watching through binoculars, had seen everything. As his friend fell, he heard the shot. Without hesitation he stripped down to his underwear and dived overboard. A powerful swimmer he soon reached the slip where his friend lay. He rushed up to Dick, carefully turned him onto his back and cradled his head.

'Where'd they get you?' he asked, then noticed the bloodstain on Dick's chest.

'I guessed right, I stopped them.' Dick coughed up blood and then continued, 'Think we can still save the slender thread?'

'I'm goin' for help, hold on mate,' Rodney told his friend before dashing up to Bill Brontwich's office. He burst inside and was astonished to see the owner of the boat yard sobbing over his daughter's body.

'Get the police! Joan's been knifed, I think she's dead,' was all he managed to stammer.

Rodney picked up the phone and dialled the emergency number.

'Police and ambulance, quick as you can, a man's been shot at Bill Brontwich's Boat Yard, Dutchville and a young woman has been stabbed.'

'Can I have your name, please sir, and your phone number?'

'What the hell does that matter? Get the police and a

couple of ambulances with medics down here now. This isn't an accident, it's probably terrorism, I have to rush to the man who has been shot.'

Without waiting for any response he put the phone down. Turning to the boat yard's owner he said, 'Sorry, can't help you, but the medics and police will soon be here. My friend is lying on the slip with a bullet in his chest, must get back to him. I suppose that car has made a getaway?' He did not wait for an answer but rushed back to his friend.

Too late. Richard Harry England was dead. Rodney sat down beside the body, wondering about those last words. Then it came to him. Half a century ago, Dick had stood for Parliament. He had argued that 'democracy hung by a slender thread'. His daughter had reminded him of it when they set out to thwart an attempt to explode an atom bomb at Den Helder. They succeeded but it had cost Sally, Dick's only daughter, her life. He recalled her dying words: 'We've saved the slender thread, Dad.'

The ambulance, the police, the security and the press all arrived in due course. Derek Catchman was amongst them. Someone had given Rodney a blue track suit to wear and an old pair of sandals. Catchman took Rodney to one side.

'Rodney MacDonald?'

'Yes.'

'I'm Derek Catchman. I am very, very sorry at what has happened. We do owe him a great deal. From what I have heard it was only by a matter of minutes that he saved the area from total disaster. If I had my way I would award him the George Medal, but I'm sorry to say that I can't have my way.' He paused, but Rodney remained silent so he continued. 'On the face of things, it looks as if he had a squabble with these other two chaps. He damaged their boat and one of them shot him. That is how it will be put to the press. My boss has made it clear that there must be no mention of any terrorist attempt on the *Montgomery* or how we were able to get onto their activity with the help of Mr England.'

He paused again but Rodney just gave a grunt. He thought Dick should be recognised for his public-spirited sacrifice, but he could also see the need for secrecy at this stage.

'We are not convinced it is all over. Someone, probably this gang, tried to nobble the diesel for the stand-by generators at Deephole nuclear power station. Fortunately one of their gatekeepers got suspicious and that was thwarted. They probably don't know that we found the adulterated fuel so they may be thinking their scheme is still on. They had spiked it with nitro glycerine which, as soon as the diesels were started up, would have put them out of action. We don't know for sure why they did this. It could be that they are planning an attack on the station so the security has been upped. We are still puzzled about the repeated reference to Guy Fawkes we've picked up. The way it has been mentioned suggests it is an operation not a pseudonym.'

'Can't help you there. Dick had no ideas about that. Well he thought from what we knew it was an attack on the House of Commons. Maybe there are two attacks planned? Maybe this is a diversion? Do you think Dick will get some official recognition when all this is over?'

'Keep mum for now and I'll see what can be done later. We don't yet know for sure that they were going for the *Montgomery* but it seems most likely. We found a metal container in the dinghy. It looked like a very large tin of paint. I've called in the bomb squad to look at it. If they were targeting the *Montgomery* then they would have needed an explosive charg...'

His words were brought to an abrupt end by a loud explosion a hundred yards or so from where they stood. The blast wave bowled them over but they escaped with just a little bruising. The depth charge had exploded while it was being moved by the bomb squad. The two officers handling it were blown to pieces, and several bystanders were injured.

Later, after the carnage had settled, Rodney got to the dinghy that his friend had tied down to the chain lining the slipway, and returned to *Rose of England*. He started tidying his friend's belongings, then gave up and crashed out on his bunk.

In the evening light, he was sitting on the after deck, a glass of wine in hand, thinking of the day's events and his lost friend. He would have to ask someone to help him take *Rose of England* back to the Deben. It would then be for the solicitors to sort out Dick's affairs. After the loss of his daughter Sally, he had no family of his own.

As these thoughts were going through his mind, his eyes scanned the shore lights and the lights of the town. He was just thinking that, but for Dick's sacrifice, they would not be there when all of a sudden the lights went out, plunging the whole area into darkness. It was just 9 pm.

Fifty miles away, in a Suffolk field, eight small explosions had fired and four pylons carrying the power from Deephole nuclear power station crashed down. They fell against each other. A massive electric explosion followed as thousands of amps flashed to earth melting the remaining pylon legs. It was like a horrendous lighting strike with an ear-splitting clap of thunder. The lines fell across the couple of cottages which lay under them. These burst into flames. Lilly Saunders and her two children, a girl aged five and a boy aged seven, were stunned by the shock wave and died in the fire. In the other cottage, Mary and Keith were just preparing for an early night in bed. Their clothes burst into flames and they staggered screaming down the stairs to the door but it had jammed shut. The fumes overcame them; they collapsed and were burnt to death. The cables fell onto the main road just as a coach with 24 pensioners on board, returning from a day's mystery tour, was passing. The falling cable trapped the vehicle which skidded, turned over and burst into flames. Only the driver and one passenger escaped with their lives.

The sudden loss of the transmission lines caused the nuclear reactors at Deephole to trip. The control rods dropped into the reactors and the nuclear fission stopped. For a few moments the station was plunged into darkness. Then the standby diesels fired up and started to generate essential power to keep the cooling-water motors running, which was necessary to avoid a reactor meltdown. The conspirators' plans to start a nuclear disaster had been thwarted. The staff on the stations, unaware of what had caused the sudden loss of the transmission lines, relaxed as they congratulated themselves.

In Somerset, two explosions caused two pylons, in an open field, to collapse into each other. The grid lost another 4 GW of supply in addition to the 6.5 GW it had lost from Deephole. The system immediately became unstable. From Lands End to the Humber the whole country lost power and was plunged into darkness. The British Grid control operators were in an impossible situation. They struggled to maintain some parts of the system. The sudden loss of such a large amount of power had made the whole system unstable; power surges and depressions caused the safety systems to shut down supplies to consumers. The grid control engineers were frustrated by the loss of power in their own area as they tried to call on power stations that had been off load to fire up and generate. A few stations were on standby, steaming and ready to generate, but others were cold. The problem that they faced was not just generating more power but how to restart the damaged system. It would take several days, time that, in the event, they would not have.

The five conspirators aboard the *Fleur de Veurne*, which was lying on the Visitors' Pontoon in Dunkirk marina, were listening to BBC Radio 4 broadcasting on 198 kHz when all of a sudden it went dead. They raised their glasses and in unison muttered, 'We did it, now let's get out of here.'

They picked up their rucksacks, walked up the pontoon and out through the gate and went their separate ways back to their home countries. Their job was done.

10

Aftermath

At 21.00 hours that evening, the load on the British grid was 35 GW. It was one of the lows but totally expected on a summer evening. The Grid Controller was expecting a surge in an hour's time when a popular television programme would be ending. A gas-fired power station was on standby to pick up the extra load. The nuclear stations at Deephole were running flat out, generating 5.5 GW. In the force 4 wind, the generators out at sea were adding another gigawatt to the power being fed into the grid at Deephole. When the pylons were blown the grid suddenly lost 6.5 GW, some 18% of its supply. The grid went unstable and areas of the country started to shut down as the Controller desperately sought to replace this lost generation. It was then that the pylons in Somerset were blown and the grid lost another 12%. With a total loss of 30% of available generation the whole system collapsed, and most of England and parts of Wales lost all their power. The country was plunged into darkness and much worse.

Out on the roads, the traffic had been moving normally. The motorways were heavily loaded with some cars ignoring the national limit and cruising along at speeds up to 100 mph. Suddenly all the installed lights went out. The complex junctions, brightly lit one moment, were plunged into twilight. Traffic control lights failed, as did the warning signs. On the M1 a fuel tanker fully laden with petrol was hit by a speeding van as it entered one of the suddenly blacked out junctions. Petrol spilt onto the road, caught fire, and then the tanker exploded. The drivers of the tanker and the van were killed instantly. The fireball spread across to the other side of the road bringing all the traffic to a complete halt.

Other vehicles managed to stop and those seeing the accident grabbed their mobile phones and dialled 999. They got no response. The emergency control centres were without power and their phone systems crashed. Chaos ensued. Massive tailbacks developed and all traffic in that area ground to a halt. This incident was not unique; others followed all over the country, on major roads out in the open areas. Crash after crash followed. People lay injured, unable to get help, unable to get anything other than very basic first aid treatment from some of the survivors with limited training.

In the towns, now in pitch darkness, all the traffic lights were out of action. Motorists exercised caution but there were still many accidents, most of them minor without involving serious personal injury. Nevertheless there were some that did require ambulance and police help but, as the control rooms were without power their systems were down, and their services not available.

The railways were brought to a halt as signals failed and even level crossing gates failed to open. The late evening express from Glasgow to London came to a halt 80 miles from its destination. It was plunged into darkness. For the first ten minutes the passengers waited for information – it did not come, nobody knew what was happening. Gradually they grew restless; some were angry, some were sleepy, some were frightened. The more adventurous started to make their way to the front and rear of the train, in the hope of finding someone who could explain the situation.

Just before the lights failed, the fellow in the grey hooded anorak had seen the chap sitting next to him put a wallet full of £50 notes inside his jacket. In the dark, he lunged his fist into the man's solar plexus then reached into the fellow's jacket, relieved him of his money, got up and stumbled along the corridor to the nearest door, opened it and jumped down. The fellow who had received the blow coughed, choked and died.

Hundreds of other trains were stranded but a few diesels, whose drivers were not immediately aware of the situation, carried on.

Johnny Drivewell was feeling tired. He had driven his low loader with its heavy 40-foot motor cruiser strapped down for nearly 80 miles, now he was nearing the end of the trip. He had been delayed with hold-ups on the motorway and also stopped by the police in a routine commercial vehicle check-up. The original plan was to deliver the boat to the yard at about 8 pm but he had phoned to tell them that his ETA would be more like 10 pm. They had agreed to leave the yard gate open for him and, although the following day would be a Sunday, they would come and unload him in the morning. Spending a night in his cab was normal practice and he was looking forward to making a cuppa and then bedding down.

He glanced at his satnav. It told him there were only another six miles to go and that in a few hundred yards there was a level crossing over a branch line. As he approached in the evening light, his headlights picked up the crossing barriers which were in the open position. He drove on, unaware that the power failure had left them like that.

The late evening diesel train was making its return journey back to its overnight stopping station some 10 miles down the track. As usual at this time of night, it was only half full of passengers. They were mainly middle-aged adults but there were some children with them and also a few pensioners. The engine driver knew the route and was looking for the green light at the crossing but as he could see nothing he thought he was not quite there. When he saw the lights of the low loader he applied the emergency braking procedure, but it was too late.

The train hit the vehicle just behind the driver's cab. The low loader skewed round, throwing Johnny from his cab onto the grass verge. He broke his leg in the fall. The train derailed and fell on its side. The driver died instantly with a broken neck. Nearly half of the passengers were killed. Most of the children survived although many were injured. A few of the surviving adults managed to scramble out. Some stopped to help the injured survivors and a couple went for help. Half a mile back along the road down which the low loader had travelled was a group of old farm workers' cottages. Some were now holiday homes but they were all occupied. The residents turned out to help and were able to accommodate the walking injured and comfort those still trapped in the train. Telephones were no longer working but using their initiative some got in their cars and went for help. Despite their best efforts, 29 people died at the scene, eight died later when they got to the local surgery, and 35 suffered debilitating injuries which stayed with them for the rest of their lives.

On the streets of the large cities, the muggers were having a field day. The revellers and those just out for an evening's entertainment were suddenly plunged into darkness as they were walking along the streets looking for a taxi or a place for another drink. When the electricity failed so did all the CCTV cameras. What happened to Janice and Winston Finebody was just one example of what lay in wait for hundreds of others. They were walking towards the multi-storey car park but they never made it. Two thugs came up from behind and bundled the pair into an alley. One held the terrified woman while the other stabbed the man through the heart. As he died the thug searched his body, removing his wallet, watch, and wedding ring. That completed, they turned their attention to the woman and tore off her clothes, threw her to the ground and removed her rings and jewellery. As they left, one turned to her and muttered, 'Think yourself lucky we didn't rape you.' He then struck her in the face leaving her semi-conscious.

The evening revellers, shoppers, show-goers were all distressed. Not only were they in darkness, but cash machines did not work. Shops that were still struggling on by torch or other light could not take credit or debit cards. Some customers tried to pay with cash but the tills would not work. Anger and chaos ruled.

All over the towns, people were trapped in lifts, and in buildings with automatic doors. Others who were ageing or had disabilities, living in the high-rise apartments, also found themselves trapped. The emergency lighting helped to ease their plight but it was never intended to deal with such a situation. Some fell down the stairs as they were attempting to get to or from their rooms. The unfortunate ones lay for hours in agony waiting for and hoping for help, which did not come until the morning. Without lifts, many of the rooms were inaccessible to the elderly or less physically fit. Generally in the buildings, from basement to rooftop, there was darkness. The residents could not even boil a kettle of water. Electric cookers were useless, fridges and freezers stopped working. Worst of all, they had no television.

Out on the streets in the larger towns and cities, gangs started to gather. They looted shops and buildings, they fought and scuffled with each other, and racial tensions came to the fore. The police, lacking proper communication and control, struggled to maintain law and order but without much success.

Those who suffered most were the sick and handicapped. Those who were dialysing or on other support machines, those who required power to give them comfort or just keep them alive. Their carers were desperate for help, but none was available and they just had to watch their charges suffer and in some cases die.

For the next few days, British Grid sought to restore supplies. The total installed generating capacity in England was some 65 GW. The loss of the two transmission lines accounted for 10.5 GW. Summer was the time of year when demand was lowest on the system and consequently it was when power stations were taken out of service for their statutory inspections and for maintenance. This, together with another station that was off line for technical problems, accounted for another 16 GW not being available. As the evening gave way to night, the wind dropped and another 15 GW from the wind farms was lost. Consequently the total available generation capacity available to British Grid the next morning was only 23.5 GW, inadequate to meet the usual night load without selective load shedding, let alone the daytime requirements The morning load was expected to rise to 40 GW and there was no way this could be met. British Grid struggled to restore supplies but England would not wait.

The situation worsened. The news of what had happened spread rapidly amongst the militant dissident groups. Transmission pylons carrying the power from other generating stations were targeted, their supporting legs blown away or cut with acetylene torches. The wooden poles carrying the low voltage cables were being cut down and the cables stolen for their scrap value. The police, overwhelmed by multiple calls for their services, were powerless to intervene.

That first evening when the lights went out, the ordinary citizen stayed indoors with windows and doors securely locked. They lit a candle or two as they went to bed, thinking that all would be restored by the morning and their telephone would be operating. They thought they would have television and radio, their electric kettle and cooker would be working and the newspaper would tell the story of why their community had been affected.

When they awoke they got a bad surprise. Things were even worse than when they went to bed. The taps were running dry and the toilets were not flushing. Their misery was compounded by the weather. A front with pouring rain was making its way slowly across the country and with pumps not operating, floods developed in places where they had not been seen before. Raw sewage was flowing around some of the streets. Those in the high rise blocks of flats were virtually imprisoned, afraid to venture out or unable to tackle the seemingly never-ending staircase.

The following morning another major difficulty arose. The fridges, now useless, were warming and the food inside required cooking. Without the electric cooker and the microwave, this presented a major problem for a lot of people. Even the gas cookers started to falter as the supply of gas weakened and finally came to an end. Some people with gardens lit fires and tried to cook on them but often with disastrous results. Some people got burnt as they tried to light their fire with petrol. In a few cases, the fire spread and set the surroundings alight. With failed water supplies, such blazes were impossible to control, and property after property was lost to the flames.

The dairy farmers and milk processing business were in

dire straits. The cows had to be milked but the milking machines, without electricity, were useless. The animals had to be milked by hand, a very slow process. Once the milk was collected, there was no way it could be pasteurised and bottled, it just had to be poured away.

In the outside world, a major part of England had come to a standstill – banks, factories, shops, offices, transport had come to a halt. In Downing Street, at numbers 10 and 11, diesel generators had been rigged and emergency meetings were in session. The British Grid Controller had been summoned to the Prime Minister's meeting but was unable to give any assurance as to when matters would return to normal. Some of the power stations that had been cold were now firing up. A breeze had sprung up and the wind generators were starting to work but the grid was in a state of unbalanced disarray. Some criminals had realised that, with parts of the grid shut down, they could approach the high voltage power lines and the three-phase lines supplying local communities. Wherever there was the opportunity, they had cut out the wires to get the copper conductor for scrap metal. The Grid Controller indicated that supply would be restored to parts of England but it would take time. Emergency generators were supplying power to the BBC, and the Prime Minister was urged to address the nation. A special land line had been set up so this could be done direct from Number 10.

In the large towns law and order broke down, and looting and fighting continued, completely overwhelming the police and army units that were available in the UK. Everywhere, anarchy ruled as people settled old scores, as gangs fought, as crowds ransacked homes, banks, factories, and even boats in the docks waiting to be unloaded. Downing Street was besieged by angry crowds who were only held at bay by armed police and a handful of soldiers. As the day wore on so the crowds became more militant. Some found weapons and the situation deteriorated. Finally, the National Emergency Committee came to a decision: there was only one way to restore law and order. The Prime Minister's hot line to the EU President in Brussels was still operating. He called up and asked for help in the form of rapid military intervention. The BBC had managed to power up their transmitters and the Prime Minister went on the air:

'This is an emergency broadcast; the contents have been agreed with the Leader of the Opposition. Due to terrorist action, a large part of our country has been deprived of electricity; some criminal gangs have taken advantage of this. The excessive demands that the situation has placed upon our police and emergency forces has made it difficult to contain these evil forces. The situation has been compounded by others who have chosen to loot shops and some private houses. I am therefore declaring martial law for the whole of England and Wales. There will be a curfew between 8 pm, that is eight o'clock in the evening until 9 am, that is nine o'clock in the morning. Anyone outside in the streets or open spaces will be arrested and if they resist arrest may be shot.

'During the day time you should stay indoors as much as possible and go outside only for essential reasons. You may shop and pay cash or give promissory notes but the electric tills will not be working. Cash points with ATMs will not be available. It is anticipated that electricity supplies will be restored in the next few days but this may not be for all areas, as the rioting and vandalism has resulted in considerable damage to the power lines. Any person found molesting the power lines, especially for the purpose of stealing the wires, may be shot on sight. Because of the excessive demands upon our own security forces, the government have asked for assistance from our European friends. You are required to give them every assistance and to obey any instructions they may give. Thank you all for your cooperation'. The Prime Minister's broadcast was repeated at frequent intervals.

The recently formed European Police Force and SWAT teams were quickly assembled. They were supported by the European armed forces. The cross Channel ro-ro ferries were requisitioned, loaded with armoured vehicles, water cannon and foot soldiers. The Channel Tunnel was also put under military command. Within hours of the Prime Minister's broadcast, these forces were landing at Dover, Ramsgate and Harwich. They first made their way to London, enforcing the martial law as they went. Looters, caught red-handed, were shot on the spot. Control points were established. Once London had been quelled, and with the terrified population sheltering in their homes, these new forces of law and order gradually took command of the rest of England. They then turned their attention to Wales, which they subdued, encountering only a little resistance. Just forty-eight hours after the disaster had struck, EU forces were in complete control of the country

Suppressed by force of martial law, the population managed as best they could. Many died and bodies were piled up everywhere. Vehicles were organised to travel round and collect the dead for mass burial. As someone was heard to remark, it was like when the Black Death had struck and carts went round calling 'Bring out your dead'. Major industries collapsed and would not recover. The Stock Market, backbone of the British economy, lost so many accounts that when it did manage to start trading it was no longer viable. Britain lost its triple A credit rating and became such a high risk that interest rates reached unsustainable levels. Britain was broken and ruined, even though British Grid did eventually manage to restore supplies to most of the affected areas.

* * *

The EU Commission was in full session and demanded their fee for restoring order in the British Isles. The Prime Minister had no choice but to concede. The Forces of Europe were already in full control of the country. It was agreed that the Royal Family could maintain their status with relation to the Commonwealth but the United Kingdom, as a nation, would no longer exist. Scotland was now an independent country in the European Union. Northern Ireland was forced to combine with the Irish Republic, while England and Wales were split up into three districts. The southern and western counties and Wales became part of France. The eastern and central counties became part of Belgium. The northern part of England became a satellite of Germany.

Richard Harry England had given his life in vain trying to save his country, his beloved England, from terrorism. He had failed – and all of Britain also died.

A French newspaper headlined:

L'Angleterre est Mort.

A German newspaper headlined:

England befindet sich jetzt in der Müllkippe.

It was an American newspaper that simply headlined it as:

The Day England Died.

A week later, Argentina took control of the Falklands.